DARKNESS

DARKNESS

CHRISTOPHER KROVATIN

SCHOLASTIC INC.

All rights reserved. Published by Scholastic Inc., *Publishers since 1920.* SCHOLASTIC and associated logos are trademarks and/or registered trademarks of Scholastic Inc.

The publisher does not have any control over and does not assume any responsibility for author or third-party websites or their content.

This book is a work of fiction. Names, characters, places, and incidents are either the product of the author's imagination or are used fictitiously, and any resemblance to actual persons, living or dead, business establishments, events, or locales is entirely coincidental.

ISBN 978-1-338-74629-7

10 9 8 7 6 5 4 3 2 1   21 22 23 24 25

Printed in the U.S.A.   40

First printing 2021

Book design by Keirsten Geise

DEDICATED TO JACOB KING, MY DREAM COME TRUE, WHO
SLEPT FITFULLY NEXT TO ME AS I WROTE THIS BOOK.

JACOB, YOU ARE THE MOON BY WHICH I SEE THROUGH
THE DARKEST NIGHT. I LOVE YOU.

1

THE ISLAND

"Get ready," said Hannah, pointing out into the gray. "Here comes a big one."

Alec found the wave she was pointing to, swollen and topped with white foam. He watched the water roll forward in a towering bulge. Just before it hit the rock spires, he did as Hannah had instructed and closed his eyes. In the blank world behind his eyelids, the wave made a *CRASH*, and for the first time he could hear what she was talking about, the deepness of the sound, how it seemed full of tinier noises, how it echoed through the dark.

Alec opened his eyes and smiled at Hannah. His friend grinned back at him, her excitement making all the freckles around her cheekbones and nose form a shallow U.

"You heard it that time, right?" she said. "The heartbeat. I *swear*, there's a heartbeat behind the way the waves crash."

"I *think* so," he said. He stared out at the white foam and dark water sucking away from the edges of Cathedral Rock, whose two tall, spiked towers climbed out of the water about a quarter mile from shore. From where Alec and Hannah sat atop the cliffs on the island's south coast, Cathedral Rock was like a set of black horns, the seabirds ducking in and out of the nests they made in the towers' surface like white ants. "Does the sound come from the stone that Cathedral's made of? All the weird pores in the surface?"

"No, you *dork*," said Hannah with an exaggerated sigh. "It's because when you starve your eyes, you can hear all the little details of it. It's about tricking your ears, not *rock science*."

Alec wanted to groan at how she said *rock science* the way some people said *cockroaches*. "Rocks are cool," he said softly.

"Yeah, I'm aware that you think that," said Hannah. "I'm going to agree with you only so you don't go further into *why*, or what *made* the Cathedral."

He couldn't help himself. "It's probably some kind of igneous rock from a volcanic—"

"I will *pay you* not to talk about rocks," said Hannah.

Alec laughed, and Hannah joined him. He liked that laugh, all the heart she put behind it. It was part of why he let her poke fun of his nerdy hobby—he knew if he really wanted to tell her about rock formations, she'd listen. She was like the island that way, hard around the edges, not *sweet* or *easy* the way places were supposed to be.

They listened to the crashing waves awhile longer, swinging their feet over the edge of the cliffs. Alec watched the swirling overcast sky and the slate-gray deep of the sea stretch off into the distance until they met with the dotted shoreline of Seattle in the distance. He felt the yawn of the cliff beneath him, the pull of the open air and the eighty-foot drop below. Then Hannah whipped out her phone—sequined to death with a giant PopSocket on the back—and checked the time.

"I gotta help my mom with dinner stuff," she said, climbing to her feet.

"Isn't it, like, eleven thirty?" he asked. "You haven't even had lunch yet."

"Yeah, but she's making stew, and that takes all day," Hannah replied. "You wanna come help? You can explore the house like a scientific weirdo." She smirked. "Or hang out with Big Gran."

Alec shuddered at the image of Hannah's spooky great-grandmother, but the thought of getting free rein to wander around her endless old house was too much to pass up.

"Count me in," he said.

They got on their bikes—Hannah's caked with scabs of rust from the seawater in the breeze, Alec's just starting to bloom with red—and rode off toward town. Alec took a deep breath of the crisp, salty air and watched the old, flaky houses of Founders Island pass him by, leaning this way and that on half-sunken foundations and rotten-wood porches. When he and

Mom had arrived on the ferry six months ago and moved into their own ramshackle, sea-sagging home, he'd been so bummed out, so angry about trading their clean white San Francisco apartment for this barnacle-covered sinkhole of a town. Now, even though he wasn't sure he *loved* the drafty old place, it was beginning to grow on him . . . like a barnacle. He'd never seen anything else like Founders Island, all gray and lopsided. And so far, he'd only seen it in winter, which was never a great time to judge a seaside town.

They sailed through the village—mostly a collection of boarded-up antique shops waiting for tourist season, though Mr. Merka waved to them through the windows of the grocery store. Then they pedaled up over the hills toward the northeast shore. They turned onto a sandy dirt road, and Alec could see Hannah's house on its hill in the distance, all gables and chimneys and shutters, like three wooden houses had crashed into one another. People in town called it the Honeycomb because of how many secret passages and small rooms ran through it. Besides examining the island's countless unusual rock formations, exploring the 'Comb was Alec's favorite thing to do here so far.

Hannah saw the stone come rolling out onto the road before Alec did, and swerved. Alec's mind tried to juggle the pieces at once—Hannah's bike skidding up dirt, the huge gray rock tumbling into their path, the laughter coming from behind a bush—but in the end he was too late.

His front wheel hit the stone, bit into it, and sent the back of his bike flying up. He had just enough time to twist his body so that he landed on his side and not his head.

Wham. A flash of white crossed Alec's eyes, and the air shot out of his lungs. The sandy road burned at his points of contact—his cheekbone, his elbow, the back of his hand, his knee. When he finally slid to a stop, he tried to scramble back to his feet but was so shocked and winded that he found he could barely move.

"Alec!" cried Hannah. He heard her bike scratch to a halt, then felt her kneeling next to him, her cool hand on his cheek. "Are you okay?"

"I think so," he croaked, trying to get his wits back. "What *happened*?"

"Yeesh, newbie, you gotta be careful!"

Alec recognized the voice and sneered. *Oh,* he thought, *that's what happened.*

Derek Rector came stomping out of the bushes by the side of the road, a smile full of braces slapped across his square head. Behind him stood the kid everyone called Checkmate, almost six feet tall at thirteen, stone-faced and pale as a sheet. Alec felt his heart sink; Derek was a jerk, but the rumors he'd heard about Checkmate were terrifying.

"What is *wrong* with you, Derek?" snapped Hannah. "He could've broken his neck, you . . ." And then she said a word that would get Alec grounded.

"Hey, falling rocks happen on Founders!" said Derek, going hard on the fake innocence in his voice. "Not my fault the newbie hasn't learned the terrain yet! Besides, I thought everyone rides a bike in China."

"I'm not from China," grunted Alec, forcing himself to shake Hannah's hands away and stand. He could feel blood oozing from the scrapes across his body, but he'd be damned if Derek saw him look weak. "I'm Chinese *American.*"

"Oh, *excuse me,*" said Derek. "Might as well be

China for us on Founders, newbie. Point is, you aren't from here, and it might be good for you to learn how to navigate the island before you ride around like you own the place. Hannah can explain—she's a lifer like me."

Alec felt Hannah tense next to him like a coiled snake, ready to unleash another string of venomous words, but he held his palm up to her—*wait*. He had something to say, a real nasty barb that he'd overheard his mom talking to their neighbors about. It wasn't very nice, and it might get him beat up, but he knew it'd stick in Derek like a splinter and get infected.

"Must be tough, huh?" he said.

"What's that?" asked Derek, looking unimpressed.

"Oh, just having all these generations of your family run a successful business here," said Alec with a tight smile, "and then to have your parents drive it into the ground."

Derek's grin disappeared, and his cheeks bloomed with red. Hannah shook her head. Checkmate arched an eyebrow.

"Watch your mouth, kid," said Derek softly. "You might get hurt, talking like that."

"You mean like those tourists did last year, on one of your dad's boats?" asked Alec.

"Checkmate, grab him," said Derek.

Checkmate calmly marched toward Alec, all long limbs and cold eyes. Hannah grabbed Alec's arm and tugged him toward her house. Alec wondered how hard he'd have to kick a guy that big to give himself a decent head start.

He felt a buzzing in his teeth, almost like electricity. Adrenaline, he wondered, or just terror?

Then everything went black.

2

DARKNESS DESCENDS

His first thought was *I've fainted. Now Derek's going to think I'm some fragile little wimp, and I won't even be able to fight back as he beats the snot out of me—*

Then he felt Hannah's grip tighten on his arm and heard Derek shout.

"Alec, I can't see," said Hannah, drawing close and gripping Alec for dear life. Alec opened and closed his mouth, trying to think of a response, but he had nothing. Everything *felt* the same, from the rough sand under his foot to the stinging on his knee to the salty breeze on his face—but all he could see was blackness, as deep and dark as any night he'd ever witnessed.

Even worse, it stayed dark. Alec kept waiting for his eyes to adjust, for faint outlines to begin rising out of the total blackness . . . but there was nothing. It was pure black, without even a glimmer of light or reflection to guide him.

"Siri?" yelled Derek. "Siri, turn on flashlight . . . Siri? Man, my phone's messed up. Checkmate, man, try yours!"

Our phones, thought Alec. His hand scrambled for his pocket and dug out his phone. He pressed the home button, and—

Nothing. Not even the glow of his home screen. Either it had died in his pocket over the course of the bike ride, or . . .

"I think it's totally dark," said Alec, partly to himself. "We can't see anything."

"Yeah, I'm sure the sun just went out, *idiot*," snapped Derek, but Alec could hear his voice warbling with more fear than anger. Anyway, Derek was right—it made no sense, that all of them had lost their sight at once. What else could it be, though? If there'd been some sort of event, a solar eclipse or an especially heavy storm, they would've heard about it online or on TV. What other answer was there?

Hannah tugged at him, and Alec reeled. The total darkness was disorienting; suddenly, he had no sense of distance and couldn't tell where anything was. His feet got tangled, and the two of them tumbled to the dirt together, Alec's scrapes crying out in pain.

"Are you all right?" he asked, fumbling for Hannah and finally grabbing her shoulder.

"I'm fine," she whispered, breathing heavy. "Look, my house is just a few yards that way. If we keep crawling, we should get there. Come on, grab my ankles."

Alec did as she said, and the two of them started crawling along the path on their hands and knees. The dirt scraped his palms, and Derek screamed and shouted behind him, but Alec forced himself to think about nothing but moving forward, crawling to Hannah's house. The house would be safe, he told himself, no matter what this was, no matter what was happening to the world.

Focusing proved hard. Without his sight, every

sound, smell, and sensation was amplified. Alec could hear things that he wouldn't have noticed otherwise—Hannah's mom shouting in their house up ahead, the soft sob Hannah put on every exhale, car horns honking and people slamming doors in town behind them. Even worse, the darkness injected his mind with fear, worries of what could be out there in the dark roaming around, watching him even though he couldn't see it. It reminded him of a time he'd gone snorkeling with his mom on vacation; they'd swum out so far that the bottom of the ocean dropped away, and he couldn't stop imagining a huge tentacle reaching up out of the depths to wrap around his neck.

All at once, he felt like a little kid again, terrified of the darkness. His hand tightened around Hannah's ankle the way it had around his mom's hand on that long swim.

"You okay?" whispered Hannah, never stopping.

"Y-yeah," said Alec, trying to sound brave through the knot in his throat.

A moment later, Hannah cried out joyfully, and then Alec felt something beneath his hands—stones, big and flat, placed together to form a line. It was the path leading up to the Honeycomb's front porch. Up ahead, he could hear Hannah's mom calling out again. They had to be close, he thought.

Then he heard a different sound.

One not made by a human.

Alec stopped mid-crawl as icy horror prickled along his arms and neck. He barely felt Hannah shake her foot beneath his hand as he tried to turn his ear just right and pick up the strange sound.

"Alec?" asked Hannah, sounding panicked. "Alec, what is it? We're almost there—"

"There's something out there," he blurted out.

Hannah paused, listening. "I don't hear anything, Alec, please, we just have to—"

Then he heard it again. This time, Hannah tensed in his grip, and he felt her heartbeat in her ankle.

Off to their left, there was shuffling noise, like something large was crawling across the grass. Only this wasn't the usual *pat-pat-pat* of a dog or cat trotting toward them but a quick, scrabbling sound, like something scaly brushing against itself as it shuffled forward. Behind it were other sounds—grunts, clicking, a wet smacking like a mouth full of peanut butter.

"What . . . what is that?" whispered Hannah.

"I don't know," said Alec. "But I think it's getting closer."

There was no doubt about it—with each second, the scrabbling got louder, until it sounded as though it was only a few feet away. This close, Alec could smell something, musty and sour like the inside of the iguana cage at their school. More than that, in the blackness around him he could *feel* it, could sense the thing coming toward them. Between the sounds and his own frightened mind, he began to paint its shape: low to the ground, too many legs, drooling mouth. *Most certainly*, he thought as he dry-swallowed, *not a mammal.*

The noises grew so loud, they were deafening. Alec felt the cold, clammy feeling inside of him swell, so big that he couldn't suck in breath around it, so huge and awful he thought he might burst. He let go of Hannah's ankle and pushed back onto his butt, scooting away from whatever was crawling in the dark.

A short distance away from him—it could've been miles, it could've been inches, for all he knew in this endless black—the sounds stopped.

Alec froze, not daring to breathe. The silence was somehow worse.

He *knew* the creature was out there, but now he didn't know where.

There was a chirping noise, almost like a low moan through a mouthful of snot.

Something feathery and slick brushed against Alec's cheek.

The bubble burst inside of him. He screamed into the night.

In an instant, it was day again.

Alec blinked hard, his body heaving with breath. Around him was the Sunday morning he and Hannah had just ridden their bikes through—overcast and windy, but perfectly ordinary. He and Hannah lay on the stone path leading up to the Honeycomb, the house looking big and ramshackle but normal as ever. A few yards away, his and Hannah's bikes lay tangled on the dirt road, and beyond that, Derek and Checkmate huddled in the grass, clutching each other. Off in the distance, a cloud of black smoke was rising from town.

Alec's mind was a blur. He looked to Hannah,

searching for an answer. When he saw her, he wondered if his own face was so pale, and his eyes so wide.

"Mom?" said Hannah. Suddenly, she leapt to her feet and sprinted up onto the porch of her house. *"Mom!"*

Alec followed, not knowing what else to do. His heart was pounding, his breath was heavy—but it seemed like everything was normal. He checked his phone, and it lit up instantly with messages from his mom, full of all caps and exclamation points.

He turned into the kitchen and found Hannah hugging her mom and dad, all of them with their eyes clenched shut. Hannah shook all over as her mom shushed her. The smell of stew was thick in the air, overpowering to Alec as he tried to take deep breaths and calm down. Somewhere off in the house, he heard Hannah's baby sister, Joan, crying.

"Is everyone okay?" Hannah stammered. "Is Joan okay?"

"Joan's fine," said her dad. "We're all fine."

Something warm and leathery brushed against Alec's cheek. He spun around with a cry.

Big Gran, Hannah's great-grandmother, sat hunched in a chair by the door, staring straight ahead. The sight of her still intimidated Alec—his grandparents had gotten soft and wrinkly with age, but at 105, Big Gran seemed to have gotten tight and hard, like a piece of Naugahyde that nothing could chew through. Her one remaining eye was milky and motionless; the other socket was a small black opening where she'd stopped wearing her glass eye years ago.

Big Gran withdrew her hand from Alec's face and rolled something between her fingers—a gray-green fluid, like butter that had gone horribly bad years ago. His hand flew to his cheek, and he felt even more of the stuff smeared across his skin. A sense memory of that wet caress in the darkness made him shudder and gag.

Big Gran sniffed her fingers, and what was left of her eyes narrowed.

"It's happening again," she sighed.

3

IN THE NIGHT

Alec gasped awake. He coughed, bent at the waist, rolled over, and knuckled his eyes. After a minute or two, the world around him faded back in—the comforter cocooning his legs, the soft whir of his ceiling fan. He pressed the torn label on the corner of his pillowcase between his fingers and sighed.

His body ached. It was the second time that night he'd woken up with a start.

It had been one long day.

His mom had cried for like an hour when he got home. She kept putting her hands on his face and pressing her lips hard together. Soon afterward, texts and emails started pouring in from people in town and at the school, checking in on Mom and him. Officer Allander, one of Founders Island's three policemen, came by the house all flustered and pale, asking if they were all right and barking for them to remain inside and lock their doors. Hard curfew of 8:00 p.m.

"What *happened*?" pleaded Mom.

"I wish I knew, Merideth," said Officer Allander, looking like he'd seen his own ghost. "All I know is that happened all over the island . . . and nowhere else."

From what Mom could piece together, all of Founders had blacked out at once. Electronic devices kept working . . . but their screens and glowing buttons couldn't be seen. The island's pets had apparently lost their minds as well, barking and hissing in total panic, so the residents knew it wasn't just a human thing, either. All light was swallowed by the blackness. A few people had even tried to light candles, but the flames wouldn't glow. People were bruised, singed, and nicked up from accidents in the dark. Cars had crashed on Marina Boulevard, the main street of town. One of the two daily ferries from the island had just launched and was nearly capsized in the panic of the passengers and the confusion of the captain.

Alec's mom had fired out a lot of explanations over dinner. Shared hallucinations. Solar flares. Maybe their bread had gotten infected with ergot, a mold that could give people terrifying hallucinations; it'd happened in medieval times, she said, in an isolated town like this. Between that and all the outlandish claims she'd heard from the neighbors, from unidentified spacecraft floating through the sky to a choir of angels singing in the distance, one thing managed to appear in every story:

People had heard large, strange things moving around in the dark.

Alec remembered Big Gran's comment when she'd wiped the slime off his cheek—*It's happening again.* He wanted to blow it off as the ramblings of an old woman who probably thought the flu was cured with leeches . . . but she'd sounded so sure of herself.

And if she recognized the smell of the stuff on his cheek, then she'd dealt with something like this before.

Without thinking, Alec's hand went to his cheek, and he shuddered in the night.

If the blackout had all been in their minds, where had the stuff on Alec's cheek come from?

Alec rolled over, looked to his dresser, and realized he couldn't see a thing.

He dry-swallowed.

His eyes weren't adjusting.

There was no light from the hallway. Or the window.

He reached for his phone on the table beside his bed. Once his fingers brushed against it, he grabbed it and pressed the home button—

Nothing.

Alec felt around the floor next to his bed until he grabbed his charger cable. He plugged in his phone.

Nothing.

A sinking feeling rolled across him like one of the waves he'd watched earlier that day.

The darkness was so impenetrable he couldn't see his hand when it was right in front of him. Slowly, he edged the hand along his bedside table, found the cord for his lamp, and fingered the wheel switch. He clicked it forward.

Nothing.

It's happening right now.

The thought boomed in his mind. Even without the electronics, he thought, it was too dark right now, darker than any night he'd ever known. Somehow, while he and most of the island were asleep, another blackout had fallen over them.

If that was true . . .

Alec thought he knew his bedroom by heart, but walking through the endless blackness was harder than he'd imagined. Everything seemed to be either farther away or closer than he thought it would be. After reaching out for his dresser and nearly falling flat on his face, he tripped over his shoes and stubbed his toe on the leg of his desk. Once he finished hopping around and softly cursing, he finally hobbled his way to the wall and felt along it until he reached the window.

He raised the window, pushed open the storm shutters—and knew he was right. Normally, he'd be able to see most of the island from his bedroom, the scraggly hills outlined by moonlight and a soft halo coming off the bar at the inn along Marina Boulevard. There weren't even stars overhead, or faintly lit clouds. Alec might as well have been looking off the edge of the earth.

He tilted his head and listened. At first, all he could hear were the usual sounds—the occasional rustling tree, the roar of the ocean, a bell from a far-off boat.

Once again, his teeth hummed in his jaw.

Then he heard the noise from that morning.

The scrabbling legs. Grass being rustled. Sharp clicking vocalizations, like the bat he'd gotten to see up close at the San Francisco Zoo. The noises grew and moved around the side of his house, until Alec could sense them, *feel* them, down on his front lawn. He wasn't sure, but from what he could hear, the thing making the sounds was huge, maybe the size of a pony or a big jungle cat.

The noise stopped.

A howl blared out into the night. Alec shuddered and hunched his shoulders at the sound—gurgling and mournful, like someone crying through a throat packed with snot. It was unlike anything he'd heard before, any wolf or jungle bird he'd seen on *Planet Earth*. He would've found it sad if it wasn't so haunting and devoid of warmth.

And it was coming from his front lawn.

In the distance, another howl answered the first. Farther off, a third howl cut through the crashing waves and whistling wind, then a fourth.

There are more of them, he thought. *Whatever these things are, there are a bunch of them out there in the dark.*

"What's going on?" he mumbled.

There was a sharp shuffle and grunt from the lawn, as though the thing had turned suddenly toward him. Somehow, Alec knew, it had heard him . . . and it was looking at him.

He reared back from the window and slammed it shut, then rushed to his bed. He huddled beneath his comforter and prayed for morning.

4

WHAT HAPPENED?

"And that's why you look so *bedraggled*?"

Alec nodded slowly at his mother. Merideth Grenier might have been the kind of person who liked using words like *bedraggled* for their dramatic flair, but this time she had a point. The skin around his eyes stung and sagged, and every exhale came out as a big sigh. He was even chewing his cornflakes slowly, his mouth too exhausted to work normally. He hadn't slept a wink after he'd looked out the window last night—but how could he have, after he'd heard that horrible sound? He was still awake when the darkness lifted, around seven in the morning. His mother had slept through it all.

Now Mom arched an eyebrow and swirled her granola with her spoon. She'd gone extra big on her colors today, Alec noted, from the jungle-print blouse to the tie-dyed scarf around her head. That meant she was in a rough mood and trying to pick up her own spirits. Color was her safe space.

"You might have been having a bad dream, honey," she said with a shrug. "After what happened yesterday, it'd make perfect sense that you had a nightmare."

"I thought of that, but I'm pretty sure it was real," said Alec. "My shoes were all kicked out of the way, and I left the shutter open. And my toe was scraped from where I stubbed it."

"That might have been a result of your bike accident yesterday," she said.

Alec nodded and shoveled cereal into his mouth. He had told his mother everything about how he'd gotten scraped up—except Derek and Checkmate's involvement. It was one of the first things Hannah had told him when he'd moved here: *On an island, everyone finds out everything. If you rat someone out,* *it'll get back to them, and that's worse for you in the* *long run.*

"And anyway, from what I hear, all of this might be as simple as *celestial phenomena*," Mom said. "There's that comet we're supposed to be able to see soon. I'm sure that's giving Earth's atmosphere a bit of the old indigestion." She glanced at her phone. "Speaking of which, you might have to wolf that down, sweetheart, or we'll both be late."

"Got it," said Alec, and stuffed his cheeks. He wasn't terribly hungry—in truth, the idea of eating more made him nauseous—but Mom's outfit seemed to be working, and he didn't want to trip her up.

The day was as gray as ever as Mom drove him across the island to school, with the twin shades of sky and ocean making the countryside look how Alec felt. But today, he noted, the typical conveyor belt of scenery (old stone wall, first lamppost in miles, house that should've been demolished years ago, repeat) was dotted with bursts of uncomfortable color. A ring of neon-orange road cones circled a downed lamppost surrounded by shattered glass. The McCarthys' house had yellow police tape fencing it off. Officer Allander leaned against his old blue police sedan, pinching the phone between his cheek and shoulder while he scribbled on a notepad. He waved at Mom and Alec as they rolled by, and Alec felt like he could see scary excitement in his darting eyes. This was new for everyone, he realized. Nothing very exciting happened in Founders outside of a hurricane. People were scared.

They pulled into the lot of Founders Academy, and Alec still couldn't believe how few kids he saw walking into the old redbrick building. He remembered showing up to junior high in San Francisco as a tornado of action, friends talking to him and comparing homework as he rushed to his locker. The academy was the only school on the island, holding kindergarten through twelfth grade, and it always looked like everyone had forgotten to set their alarms.

They headed toward the door. Over it hung Miss Mary, an ivory carving of a woman that had once decorated the bow of an old ship. Alec had always found the statue creepy, with its hands clutched over its heart and its calm eyes staring off in the distance. Now he remembered Big Gran's comment and wondered if

Miss Mary had seen the sky turn black before. He could almost read it in her calm face.

It's happening again.

Mom gave him a forehead kiss and peeled off toward the art studios at the eastern end of the building. Hannah sat ahead of him on the stone stairs to the second floor, where the junior high classes were. She bobbed her head gently to whatever was on her headphones, mouthing every third word, until she saw Alec.

"I've decided I like Cardi B," she said, pulling out her earbuds. "Have you ever seen her live?"

Alec shook his head and laughed. "Not everyone from the mainland goes to Cardi B concerts every night. That's like meeting someone from France and asking if they know Bob."

"You just never knew how lucky you had it," she countered. "If someone had told you that you'd be moving to Founders, you'd have gone to see Cardi B five nights a week." She put her phone away and stood. "Everyone okay on your end? Your mom okay?"

"We're fine," he said. "It's super weird driving through town, though. Looks like a lot of people had accidents in the dark. This is a big deal, huh?"

"Alec, you have *no* idea," said Hannah. "This is easily the weirdest thing that's ever happened here. Founders Island's natural state is *boooring*. Something like this is totally bonkers."

"It sounds like Big Gran might have seen something like this before," he said, and explained the comment that Hannah's great-grandmother had made to him.

"Yeah, but Big Gran's a hundred and five years old," said Hannah. "She says a lot of cryptic stuff. When I told her I was getting a smartphone, she said, *It's only a matter of time now.*"

"There's something else, though," he said, and told her about the previous night, how he'd woken up in another blackout and had heard the scrabbling things in the dark howling at one another. Hannah listened wide-eyed and made them stop just short of their homeroom so he could finish his story.

"Creepy," she said. "So this might be happening regularly. It might be more than just an isolated incident."

"I think so," Alec whispered. "I don't know how often, but I think it's going to keep happening. And it seems like those . . . whatever those things are out in the dark, now they know that they're not alone—"

A shoulder slammed into Alec's back, sending him stumbling forward. He looked up in time to see Derek passing him, Checkmate loping silently at his side.

"Watch it, you slug," shouted Hannah.

"Consider it orientation," said Derek. "Next time, you'll get out of the way."

Alec sighed, watching him go. "I wish I knew what to say to make him back off."

"You did okay yesterday," said Hannah, "though I gotta warn you, that one won't do you any favors if people overhear you. Derek's, you know, a *lifer*."

"Like you," said Alec.

Hannah sneered like she tasted something bad. "Whatever, sure. Point is, people feel bad that his folks can't keep their business afloat." She smiled a little. "No pun intended."

"My dad would know what to say," mumbled Alec. "He would give that jerk a piece of his mind."

Hannah nodded but said nothing.

They headed to their desks, and one by one the other nine kids in their grade piled in, looking about as tired as Alec. Missy Gordon had a bruise along one of her shins, while Greg Walia rocked a nasty-looking black eye that was almost swollen shut. "I tripped and hit a banister post, all right?" he said to the whole class before anyone could ask.

Mr. Jakka came in last, small and hunched but so full of energy that he seemed to burst out of his sweater vest. Alec knew he was lucky he'd gotten Jakka for his first year at Founders—the guy was lively and funny, if a little strange. He also taught social studies, which was a subject that Alec actually liked; almost every teacher at the academy taught a homeroom and at least one other subject. According to Mom, when she'd applied for her job, Principal Zelig said, "Well, now we have an art department. Any chance you speak French?"

"So, look, guys, let's not fool around here," Mr. Jakka began. He had his trademark oomph, but today he seemed a little more serious than usual. "All regularly scheduled classes are canceled. We're going to talk about what happened yesterday, how you're feeling about it, what to do if it happens again. So." He clapped his hands. "Yesterday. Something happened. What was it? None of us know. But there are some possibilities that I wanted to share with you."

"My mom says it was a warning from God," said Margaret Geraldi.

Mr. Jakka shrugged. "Look, I'm not going to speak for God. Dude does amazing work. BUT I think there might be other explanations. First things first, guys, where do we live?"

"An island?" said Greg Walia.

"Exactly," said Mr. Jakka. "Brutal shiner you got there, Walia."

Greg sighed. "I tripped and hit a banister post."

"That'll do it," said Mr. Jakka. "So, islands. What can you tell me about islands?"

Through his exhaustion, Alec perked up and raised his hand. This was actually right up his alley.

"Yes, Xiang. Go go go."

"There are continental and oceanic islands," he said. "Founders Island is an oceanic island, meaning that it's a freestanding piece of rock out in the ocean. It's most likely volcanic in origin."

"*Serious* island knowledge here," said Mr. Jakka, pointing to Alec. "Right on, Mr. Xiang, but not what I was getting at. What I was going to say is that islands are out here in the middle of the ocean, so they experience things that don't hit the mainland. The storms are bigger, the stars are brighter, and the people—well, look at us." The class laughed. "So how could being out here on an island have caused what happened yesterday?"

"It was astrological," said Hannah.

"Here we go," said Mr. Jakka. "Ms. Maplethorpe, drop some knowledge."

"Well, my grandma said she saw the northern lights out here once," said Hannah with a shrug. "Maybe this far out into the water, away from city pollution, we can see things most people can't."

"Boom!" said Mr. Jakka. He went to the board and scribbled *Rarely visible astrological phenomenon*. "That's number one on my list of what probably happened yesterday. Well done, Ms. Maplethorpe. Founders lifer for the win."

Hannah's cheeks flushed, blurring her freckles. Alec knew she was self-conscious about being what locals called a *lifer*, meaning five generations or more of her family had lived on Founders Island—even if he didn't understand why. It was better than being a *newbie* like him, that was for sure.

"Now, what's an astrological phenomenon—yikes,

okay, real mouthful there," said Mr. Jakka. "What's a *sky thing* that could've caused what happened yesterday? Anyone? Takers?"

"The comet?" said Missy Gordon.

"Is that a question?" asked Mr. Jakka.

"The comet," said Missy.

"Bingo," said Mr. Jakka. "In the next couple of days, we'll be getting a chance to witness Erickson's Comet. First time it's been visible in almost a hundred years. Discovered by?"

"Rochester Erickson," said the class as a whole. Even Alec knew that one; he couldn't escape talking about the comet since they'd moved.

"Rochester Erickson," echoed Mr. Jakka, "first settler of Founders Island, not to mention pioneer, amateur astrologer, and a pretty decent poet." He spun his hand and stuck up his chin. "*And on this isolated rock, we see the vistas of her dreams*, as his famous verse about our hometown goes. But, okay, so: It could be astrological. Could be the comet interfering with our visibility. What else could it be?"

As Jakka started to discuss how the weather patterns of an island could've caused the blackout, Alec turned to whisper something to Hannah—and froze. His friend had lost her blush entirely; instead, she suddenly looked pale, and her brow was bunched over her green eyes. She stared straight ahead, her lips moving softly as she mouthed silent words.

"Hannah?" whispered Alec. "Dude, you okay?"

"I think Big Gran was onto something," said Hannah. "Follow my lead when they let us go for lunch."

5

DARK AS A DUNGEON

After going over the possible causes of the blackout, Mr. Jakka had the class talk about everyone's personal experiences and how they felt (*"I tripped and hit a banister post,"* sighed Greg Walia when it got to him). After that, they outlined a plan in case the blackout happened again—Mr. Jakka would do a roll call, call out for anyone in the hallway, and then all students would sit down on the floor and try to wait it out. Alec guessed that his teacher hadn't felt the brush of some strange, slimy appendage on his cheek the previous day.

A little before lunch, Mr. Jakka let them go for first break, about twenty minutes when they were allowed to grab their lunches and go to the bathroom. It was then that Hannah nodded at Alec and quickly left the room. A few minutes later, Alec followed and found her standing at the head of the stairwell, motioning for him to follow.

They were silent as Hannah led Alec down past the first floor to the basement level. A door read PRIVATE—EMPLOYEES ONLY, but when Hannah tried it, it wasn't even locked.

She waved him into a narrow passageway surrounded by a maze of plumbing and boiler parts that stank of moldy cloth and sulfur. The bare bulbs overhead were losing their battle against the shadows all around them, the light coming from them looking dingy and yellow. Alec felt a surge of excitement tinged with fear, that internal tension that came from being somewhere forbidden, doing something that would probably get him in trouble.

"How do you know your way around here?" he whispered, his voice echoing between the pipes and fuse boxes all around them.

"It's a whole thing when you grow up here," she said. "The dungeon's right up ahead."

"The *dungeon*?"

"We just call it that," she said. "It's not really a dungeon." Under her breath, she mumbled, "Anymore."

After what felt like forever to Alec, twisting and turning through the pipes, they reached an old metal door at the far end of the basement with a small barred window toward the top. Hannah pushed it slowly open, and they slipped into an old chamber with stone floors and walls, barely visible by the light coming in from a window that looked out onto the grass of the school's back lawn. The floor and walls were basalt stone, Alec noted, patched together with a paste called *daub* that was once used on houses. (*One point for geology*, he noted mentally.) Except for an old rusted filing cabinet and a shelf in one corner piled with cleaning solutions and paper towels, it looked to Alec as though the room had come right out of the 1800s, older than any part of the island he'd seen before (and that was saying something).

"So before it was a school, this building used to be the Founders Island town hall," explained Hannah, her voice echoing loudly in the stone room. "This room was the cell they'd keep prisoners in."

"Whoa," said Alec. "So it *was* a dungeon."

"It gets creepier," said Hannah. She walked over to the filing cabinet, its surfaces mostly eaten with rust. In the stone above it, Alec could see someone had carved words. "Mr. Jakka reminded me. The first settlers carved Rochester Erickson's hymn into the wall of the dungeon, as a way to, like, inspire prisoners toward a higher purpose."

Alec got in close and read. Sure enough, it was the poem he'd read in English class when they'd first talked about the comet, Erickson's declaration of love for the island.

Founders Hymn

When you lay down your weary head
And hear the roaring of the waves
May even hearts of flint prepare
To make this glor'ous place their graves

For Founders holds us in her hills
And bathes us in her pools and streams
And on this isolated rock
We see the vistas of her dreams

"How'd you know this was down here?" asked Alec.

"Back in the day, kids used to come down here and spend the night," said Hannah. "It was like—what's it called?—a *rite of passage*. My dad said that he and his friends slept overnight down here and swore he heard a ghost crying."

"That's super creepy," said Alec. His skin crawled at the idea of laying his head down on the clammy, moldy stone floors. "Glad that went out of style."

"Well, but I did it," she said.

"You did?" Alec asked. "Why would you ever do that? At least your father got peer-pressured into it."

"Because I wanted to be tough, and be, whatever, an *old-school lifer* like my dad," she said, folding her arms and shrugging. "Me and Derek and one of the others, Laina Ferben, came down here to spend the night. They chickened out, but I made it the whole night."

"You're so hardcore," said Alec. "But that doesn't explain what this has to do with the blackouts."

"Okay, so, when I was sitting down here, I got really bored," she said. "So I started reading the hymn and trying to memorize it. And that's when I saw that there were other words under it . . ."

Hannah grabbed the filing cabinet and pushed it to the one side with a grunt, the metal of the bottom making an awful squealing noise against the stone floor. Alec saw she was right—there were more words, another whole verse of the hymn. He leaned toward the wall—and a flash of legs sent him stumbling back with a surge of disgust.

"Ugh," he cried as the spindly creature crawled up the wall.

"Calm down—it's just a spricket," said Hannah. She put a hand against the wall in front of the bug and let it crawl into her palm. "They're harmless."

"They still freak me out," said Alec, trying to tamp down his willies. He'd never heard of cave crickets before he and Mom had moved. One night he'd made the mistake of going down to their basement after dark, and when he'd flicked on a light, they were everywhere, all spindly legs and hunched, horrible backsides. They didn't bite or sting, despite the fact that their legs made them look like spiders (which was why Hannah used the nickname *sprickets*). Instead, they just hung around basements eating old fabric and looking for water. It was like they existed *just* to creep Alec out.

Alec looked at the little creature in Hannah's hand and had to swallow his dread. He didn't like bugs, but especially disliked these ones. His dad had always been his hero, clearing his room of any roaches or wasps that found their way in during the summer. Since he'd left, Alec had felt especially helpless against them.

"Here you go, little guy," said Hannah, bringing the cricket to the barred window of the door. Once she'd flicked it out of the room, Alec felt his pulse go down a bit, and focused on the extra verse carved in the wall, hoping it would take his mind off how many bugs were probably down in the basement with them.

And through these visions of the past
We can take on the Master's plight

And dwell beneath His watchful eye
Within a cloud of endless night

"Yikes," said Alec. "No wonder we don't learn that part in class." He read the words again, and they began to click into place in his mind. "'A cloud of endless night'— that definitely sounds like what happened the other day, though there wasn't much peace going on. You think this happened to Erickson's people back in the day?"

"Otherwise, it seems like a weird thing to include in your grand hymn about the land you've discovered," said Hannah.

"Who do we think the Master is?" asked Alec.

"God, probably?" said Hannah. "But then again, most of the church art I've seen doesn't show God's people living in eternal darkness."

"Good point," said Alec. He scratched the back of his head and thought about the verse. Maybe Erickson knew about what was going on . . . but he'd discovered Founders Island long ago. If it happened to him, and it hadn't happened since, then why was it happening now—

A buzzing sensation ran through Alec's teeth, like faint electricity.

"Whoa," said Alec.

"What?" asked Hannah.

"It just . . . it feels like the last time," he said.

Hannah furrowed her brow—and all at once, the room fell into darkness.

6

NOT ALONE

"Oh *no*," whispered Hannah.

Alec checked his phone—no light, no response.

Just like that, they were in another blackout.

"Reach out for me," said Alec. He extended his hands in the darkness, feeling the same dizzying vertigo he'd had while trying to find his way around his room at night. After a few stumbling moments, he felt Hannah's fingertips graze his shoulder, and the two clutched each other for dear life.

"Terrific," said Hannah.

"At least we're inside this time," said Alec, clutching Hannah a little harder than he'd intended to. He was genuinely thankful, though—before, out by Hannah's house, it had felt like an entire world full of monsters and psychos could close in on him. Here, with his voice echoing on the stone, there was comfort knowing that it was just him and Hannah.

"Yeah, except now, not only are we stuck down here without anyone knowing where we are," said Hannah, "but we have to get through all those pipes and stuff to get back upstairs."

"We should probably just wait until it passes," said Alec, feeling the darkness yawning around him and hating the idea of venturing out into it.

"Yeah," said Hannah, and then added, "Unless . . ."

"Unless what?" asked Alec.

"Unless they send someone looking for us," she said.

Alec hadn't even thought of that. Mr. Jakka had talked about roll call if another blackout occurred, and he was definitely the kind of hardcore, high-energy teacher to think he could head out into the dark and find them. He could picture it now—*Walia? Great.*

Geraldi? Nice. Xiang? Maplethorpe? Anyone seen those two? Hokay, it's search party time.

"Okay," said Alec. "Think you know your way through this basement well enough that we could find our way out of here?"

"Maybe," said Hannah, sounding totally unsure to Alec. She took a deep, sharp breath. "I think we should try it. Otherwise, who knows how long we'll be down here? And how upset the teachers will be?"

Alec weighed their options. One option: stay here, hope the lights came back on soon, pray Mr. Jakka didn't get lost in the dark looking for them. The other option: go for a walk, bump into some pipes like an idiot, get to the stairs. He hated the idea of leaving the room and wandering off into the dark . . . but was this any better?

He swallowed hard. "Okay," he said, "but you go first."

He and Hannah edged up to one of the room's cold, damp stone walls, and then shuffled their way along it until they found the door. Hannah pushed it open, and a mixture of warm air and radiator smell hit Alec in the face. The basement was still full of clicks and clanks and the rush of water through pipes, but it was much more sinister in the total darkness.

Inch by inch, Hannah shuffled forward, with Alec clinging to her so tightly that he could smell her fruity shampoo. Hannah was actually doing all right at navigating, remembering two turns when they showed up, all the while mumbling, "I think we're good . . . I think we're good . . ." It was fine, he reminded himself. They were down here alone, just him, Hannah, and . . .

The cave crickets.

Icy fear sliced through Alec at the thought. They *loved* the dark, creeping around at night where no one could see them. Whenever his mom put out sticky traps for them, none of them caught anything during the day, but in the morning he'd go down to the basement and find them bristling with huge, dead legs. He told himself to focus on following Hannah and getting out of here, and not think about thousands of cave crickets swarming around them in the dark, excited to crawl up his pant leg, up his back, through his hair, into his *mouth*—

A sound of skin hitting metal broke his terrible daydream. Hannah cried out and jerked in Alec's arms, her yelp ringing sharply off the metal pipes around them.

"You okay?" he asked.

"Fine," she said. "I just touched a really hot pipe is all. Dang, that hurt."

"Want to keep going?" he asked.

"Yeah. As long as we've started, we should see it through—"

A howl, haunting and warbling, echoed through the pipes up ahead. Alec felt his hair stand on end, and his hands gripped Hannah so hard he knew he'd have to apologize later.

It was the same howl from last night. The one made, and answered, by the thing on his lawn.

When it stopped, there was a moment of silence thicker and more tense than anything Alec had ever felt before.

"What was that?" asked Hannah.

As though answering, the hallways exploded with the sounds of scrambling legs and wet grunts. The noise grew, rounded a corner—and then came charging right at them.

"Run!" cried Alec. Suddenly, he was in the lead,

barreling down the hallways, bouncing off pipes left and right. The sounds of their footfalls and the creature's frantic rush were deafening in the contained space, making their blindness all the more complete. Alec felt his hand singe against a hot water pipe, and his hip cried out with pain when it caught a low-hanging fuse box, but he barely felt the pain, his mind crackling with the knowledge that it was getting closer, that it would be on them in seconds . . .

He felt them cross into the dungeon room—the air was cooler, the smell more like cold stone than hot rust. Once Hannah moved past him, Alec swung the door shut as quickly as possible. Both of them put their backs against it, panting with exertion.

BAM!—whatever the creature on the other side was slammed into the door, making it leap behind them. Alec nearly flew to the floor, but managed to keep himself pressed up against the old metal. The thing tried again and again, throwing itself against the door while shrieking and clicking into the darkness.

After a third try, it stopped and went quiet. Alec waited, listening to the silence on the other side.

Slowly, he raised his head and turned his ear to the barred window—

There was a wet slapping sound, and Alec felt hot breath against his ear and smelled the same rotten stench he'd smelled the day before. Moist lip smacks and throaty gurgles echoed around them. Whatever this thing was had its face pressed against the window and was trying to either get their scent or get a taste of them.

"Leave us alone!" shouted Hannah. Alec felt her arm move against him, and then heard the *DUNK* of her fist collide with the bars of the window.

On the other side, the creature screeched in pain, then stopped with a snort. Alec heard it smack its lips a few more times . . . and then it scrabbled away, the sounds of its great body moving against the pipes growing fainter and fainter until they died out altogether.

For how long they stood with their shoulders against the door, Alec couldn't say—it felt like hours, though it could've been seconds. But just like the day before, the world returned to normal all at once. Alec squinted as the gray light from the window reappeared, feeling especially strong to him after he'd been in the dark for so long. Through the door's window, he could hear the clicking and whirring of the school's boiler and electrical systems, not the grunting and the screeching of the creature that had attacked them. It was like nothing had happened.

As they left the room, Hannah shut the door behind them—and gasped.

In the metal of the door were scratches, shallow but long, and mostly in pairs. The whole surface was covered with a crosshatch of them. Around the barred window was a smear of slime similar to what Alec had found on his face.

"I don't even want to know why it was trying to get to us," said Hannah in a hollow, sad voice.

Alec nodded—but something else bothered him. Something that scared him even more, though he didn't understand why.

Never mind why it tried to get to us—why did it leave?

7

Voices in the Dark

It was all of five minutes after his mom had left for the town meeting the next night that Alec heard a rock against his windowpane. He glanced out, and sure enough, Hannah waited down on the path leading to their door, straddling her bike. Alec dropped his book, ran downstairs, and grabbed his own bike off their porch.

"Have you heard anything since yesterday?" asked Alec as they rode off toward the church.

"Nothing," said Hannah. "My mom said that today wasn't as bad as yesterday, because most people were already freaked out and stayed indoors. But apparently there were some early tourists on the ferry, and they got spooked real bad."

Alec couldn't blame them. They'd been let out of school early the day before because of how shaken everyone had been by the blackout. And it wasn't just the students, though plenty of them were crying and scared as they left; word around school was that Mr. Glibben, the music and Spanish teacher, had a total panic attack, refusing to leave the rehearsal room. He was one of several people who claimed they'd heard "big, nasty things" moving around the school in the dark.

Since then, there'd been another blackout last night, and one again today in the afternoon, both of which Alec had spent in his room. When that one had ended, word went around the island about the emergency town meeting. People wanted to know what the mayor intended to do about this.

"And you're sure it's okay we go?" Alec asked now.

"I mean, *technically* no," said Hannah. "But if we get caught, the most we'll get is a talking-to.

My family's got a lot of sway on the island. And my mom and dad won't mind." She shook her head. "My poor folks, man. My baby sister *just* started sleeping through the night, and now this happens. It's *cray*."

"Not to be rude, but this is for your own good: Nobody says *cray* anymore," said Alec. Alec watched her store the pop culture tidbit in her mind, nodding as though he'd explained a Greek tragedy to her.

St. Brendan's rose in the distance, its whitewashed steeple looking brighter than it probably was against the gray sky and woods behind it. Usually, the parking lot outside had a peppering of cars; this evening, it was jam-packed, with vehicles lining the side of the road leading up to it. Alec wondered if the whole town was here.

Hannah waved them toward a dirt path that led to the back of the church. As they rode, Alec's eye was drawn to the thick, shadowy forest behind the building, which led up to the strange sloping edge of the mountain locals called Hobble Ridge. He'd been dumbstruck by the unusual rock formation when he'd first moved here—no points or peaks, no gradual slope, just a perfect arced ridge rising out of the island. He'd wanted to wander through the woods around it, maybe even climb Hobble and figure out what had caused its unusual smoothness, but it had always been too cold before, and even as spring had rolled in, Hannah had balked at the idea of "counting rocks all day." Now he wondered if he'd ever get a chance to check it out, or if he'd spend the rest of his life on Founders Island afraid of the next possible blackout.

They tried a door leading into the church and found it locked, but a second, uglier door with chipped paint that led down to the basement was open. "This is better anyway," said Hannah, walking them through a dark hallway and into a dim, brick-walled stairwell. They took the dusty metal steps up two flights and came out of a door next to the organ, its pipes like the fan of some brass peacock.

From up on the balcony, Alec saw the church was filled with everyone from town; the pews were so tightly packed that countless people he recognized stood shifting impatiently in the aisles. In front of all of them, Mayor Friedmont leaned over the pulpit in a sharp-edged pantsuit, nervously palming down her short gray hair with one hand while holding a wireless mic with the other.

"If we can all remain calm," said Mayor Friedmont, "I think we can find an easy solution to this issue. But I do have to ask that you remain as calm as possible."

"What's going on?" someone shouted from the crowd. "Do you have *any* idea?"

"We are . . . currently working with scientific and history specialists to determine exactly what the problem is with these, ah . . . blank spots."

The crowd rumbled angrily.

"So that's a no?" shouted the same voice.

The mayor took a deep breath that the speakers around the building made perfectly audible. Alec could hear a deep quiver of exhaustion, embarrassment, and hopelessness in her voice, and he felt sorry for her.

"Right now, we're going to begin with a quarantine and curfew," she continued. "It appears as if these things have happened both between eleven thirty in the morning and one in the afternoon, and eight thirty at night through until about four in the morning. So right now, we're going to ask that everyone stay inside, with their doors locked, during those hours—"

"You want my kids to come home from school every day at lunch?" shouted a woman who Alec recognized as Greg Walia's mom. "And what am I supposed to do, just leave work and pick them up?"

The mayor nodded, almost to herself. Alec could see her forehead glisten from where he stood on the balcony.

"Well," she said, "until we have things under control—and this is for the public safety, mind you, the safety of our children—we will be postponing all classes at Founders Academy." The crowd rumbled in response. The mayor swallowed and continued. "We'll also be asking most local businesses to remain closed until—"

The roar of the townsfolk overwhelmed her. Several people stood up, yelling words that Alec couldn't make out but which sounded impolite.

"You expect us not to work when you don't even know what's going on?" screamed one man.

"It's almost tourist season!" bellowed Derek's dad, Herman.

"I told you that wireless internet was a thing of evil," shrieked Beth, Margaret Geraldi's mom, "but *no*, you all just *had* to have your *Tiger King*—"

"Everyone!" snapped Mayor Friedmont, cutting

off the commentary in the pews. She hunched over in the pulpit, gripping the edge with her free hand. "See, this? This is what I'm talking about. Right now, we're doing exactly what we've been doing the past two days, wandering around in the dark, screaming and hoping someone will come help us. But right now, we're exactly where the people of Founders have always been—out here, *alone*, making our own rules. So until we know more, we need to help ourselves, and each other. And I promise you, step one is staying inside, locking our doors, and keeping our kids home."

A ripple of whispers moved through the crowd. Someone raised a hand.

"Yes, Angelo?" asked Mayor Friedmont.

"I heard that this might have happened before," asked Angelo De Lima, the local bank teller. "Is that true? Do you know what they did then?"

The mayor sighed and nodded slowly, obviously grateful to finally have an answer to someone's question. "Yes, actually, we do have some proof of that," she said. "Mr. Blackwing can clear that up."

A figure Alec hadn't even noticed rose from a folding chair behind the mayor. The man was slender and graceful, with clothes a little too big for him and long black hair hanging around his head like a curtain. The mayor handed him the mic, and the new guy hopped up to the pulpit with an impressive spring in his step.

"Who's that?" whispered Alec. "I've never seen the guy before."

"Andre Blackwing," said Hannah. "My dad says he's a historian who's doing some sort of study about the island. He only got here last month."

"Hel*looo*, Founders! Are you ready to *rock*?" said Blackwing, a tiny smile on his face. He paused, looking around the silent crowd. "No laugh? Okay, got it, all business. The good news is, we *do* have proof of this happening before on Founders Island."

"How is that good news?" asked someone in the audience, salty and impatient.

Mr. Blackwing chuckled. "Well, because it means this isn't *entirely* new. It's not like this is something that's never happened and we should all be fearing for our lives." He pulled a rolled-up packet of papers from his back pocket and smoothed them out on the pulpit in front of him. "Okay, first up, about three hundred years ago, the Quinault people on the mainland referred to Founders as the *'island of night,'* and wouldn't go anywhere near it. Then late in the nineteenth century, one of Rochester Erickson's party, a woman named Sarah Gurant, wrote that she *'feared these long, random stretches without light,'* but that *'with a generation, they subsided.'* Finally, about a hundred years ago, we've got a couple of diary entries about strange losses of sunlight, and green glowing things moving around in the dark. But they stopped after a week." He looked up from his papers and nodded. "So."

The crowd was silent, waiting. "So *what*?" Derek's dad shouted, finally.

"So, it sounds like this has happened before, and we can rest easy knowing it's supposed to go away," said Blackwing.

"And what are we supposed to do until then?" shouted Derek's dad.

Mr. Blackwing sucked air between his teeth and gave an embarrassed shrug. "We . . . wait it out?"

The crowd erupted into noise, half of them muttering to one another, the other half yelling at Blackwing. It was all a lot of gibberish to Alec, but he could make out one phrase that was said over and over: *tourist season*. Obviously, this newcomer didn't understand how the island worked. He didn't understand that by Memorial Day weekend, this place needed to be crawling with beachcombers, sunbathers, hikers, cyclists, antiquers, and anyone else willing to spend money on the island. He didn't realize that without that tourist money, there'd be no gas bills and dinner on the table and Christmas presents, and leave it to a newbie to not get it, and who the heck did this scientist think he *was*?

The noise reached a fever pitch. One or two people got out of their pews and began walking toward the pulpit, pointing and shouting. Mayor Friedmont stepped forward, holding her palms up as though to say, *Whoa, okay, calm down*, but Blackwing just sort of smiled back at the townsfolk, unbothered.

Hannah nudged Alec's shoulder and nodded to the stairs. They headed down together and out into the evening, which had become blue and shady, with a soft chill running through the wind.

"That was intense," said Alec. "Maybe we should've stayed for the fight."

"Ah, if I want to watch one of my mom's high

school friends take a swing at a newbie, I can hang out by the tavern at the inn," said Hannah, but Alec could hear that her heart wasn't in the wisecrack. She stared off toward the cliffs, her arms wrapped around her middle, and chewed her lower lip.

"What's up?" he asked.

She shook her head slowly. "Look, fair enough, those people in there are loud and ridiculous . . . but they're *right*. We can't *wait it out*. One bad tourist season, and the island could sink. I mean, not literally, but you know, it'd be ruined."

"So what do you want to do?" asked Alec.

"I don't know," said Hannah. "I just wish we could figure out what's going on with the blackouts. Why they're coming, when they come. Obviously, all our parents have no idea why."

Alec couldn't argue with that. Everyone in town was too busy looking down the barrel of their mortgages to really care *why* the whole island was being plunged into darkness twice a day. And one thing science had taught him was that the only way of overcoming an obstacle was to know what you were dealing with.

"We could do a research session," said Alec.

Hannah arched an eyebrow. "Meaning?"

"I stay over at your house tomorrow night," he said. "During the blackout, we find ways to monitor the room around us. Start researching the blackouts from inside of them. Come up with some data."

Hannah nodded slowly and smiled. "What do you know?" she said. "Our answer lies on the nerdy path. If only it involved geology."

Alec rolled his eyes. "It's so *cray*, right?" They got on their bikes, rode out into the evening, and over the air whistling past them, they made plans.

8

READY OR NOT

"Careful with that one," said Mom as Alec hoisted the pot out of the back of their car and up to his chest. "I will be," he replied, but inside he wondered why she even bothered reminding him. Wasn't he supposed to be careful with *all* her pots? What was he going to do, roll this one down the street?

Mom grabbed two more pots—one painted in radiant blue spots and the other gray and cloudy, as though covered with a storm—and walked them to

High Tide, the one art gallery on Founders Island. Part of him wondered what they were even doing here, filling a closed gallery with Mom's handiwork for a showcase that would probably get canceled, but he knew not to say anything. Between the divorce and the stress of the move, Mom had thrown herself entirely into her art, and there were so many pots around their house at this point that he was having a hard time finding a place to put down his drink. The folks at High Tide were doing them a favor, honestly.

Alec had thought the gallery looked depressing the first time he'd seen it, its dirty windows showcasing watercolors of pebble beaches that wouldn't sell until summer, if at all. Now, with the lights turned off and the windows showing only wooden and wire art stands, it looked like it had survived the apocalypse. Genevieve, the heavyset, curly-haired woman who ran the place, half waved to him as he passed. Alec could see the worry in her face and the way she kneaded her hands. She was thinking the same thing as everyone else—*What if the blackouts don't stop? What if I can't pay my bills, and have to give up my whole life?*

Once they'd dropped all of Mom's pots off at High Tide, Mom dug around in her purse and handed Alec a twenty.

"For your sleepover," she said. "But no junk. Just because *some parents* let their kids eat ice cream all night doesn't mean I'm going to."

Alec felt his guts sink a foot. He took the money and walked away in silence, trying not to dwell on Mom's weird, loaded comment.

Some parents.

She'd wanted to say *your father*. Who else could she be talking about? Not Hannah's parents. Eating ice cream at midnight was Dad's routine—any time Alec had a friend sleeping over, Dad would come home with all the best stuff piled in his arms. Burritos, pizza, gummies, ice cream . . . It was like Dad could read Alec's mind, and knew exactly what he and his friends were craving. Mom would always just watch silently while her tray of healthy snacks was instantly forgotten.

Alec wished she hadn't brought it up. When he got to Merka's Grocery Store, he considered loading up on the sweetest and most chocolate-coated stuff available, but that felt gross and weird. He pictured Dad's smile when he came through the door, only now it felt mean-spirited, and in the background was always his mother's tired frown as she scooped up her apple slices and whole-wheat pretzel sticks.

He finally settled on a big bag of chips, some trail mix that went heavy on the M&M's, and a sixer of glass-bottle Cokes. When he got to the counter, old Mr. Merka rang him up with a tight, speedy smile.

"Having yourself a little blackout party?" he asked.

"Something like that," said Alec, trying to smile back.

"Just be inside early!" said the peanut of a man. He looked over Alec's shoulder. "Ah, young Mr. Berger! Didn't hear you come up."

Alec frowned and glanced over his shoulder. Berger? He didn't know anyone named Berger on the island—

He froze, and without meaning to his mouth fell open.

Checkmate loomed overhead, staring down at him with that long blank face. This close, Alec could see the whites of the kid's unblinking eyes, the veins on his huge hands, the tiny scar on his lip, which Hannah had heard was from a knife fight. Beneath the kid's massive form, Alec felt frozen, as though staring up at a building that threatened to fall on him at any moment.

"Yo, Checkmate, you get the soda?" called Derek's voice from somewhere in the store.

Checkmate lifted a two-liter of Sprite and slammed it down on the counter like it weighed less than a pound.

The motion snapped Alec out of it. He grabbed his snacks and ran, feeling the huge, silent boy's eyes at his back.

"Oh yeah," said Hannah. "His name's Eli Berger. You didn't think his mom named him *Checkmate*, did you?"

"Well, no one's called him anything else around me," countered Alec, twisting his shoulders and trying to get comfortable against the ultra-shaggy neon-green pillow Hannah had offered him. Her room looked like the set of a bad Disney tween movie, all posters of musicians with their names in gum-bubble font and sequins, stars, rhinestones, and extra fluff covering every surface. She tried so hard to be *mainland*, Alec knew, to look and feel like a typical American girl her age and not some scruffy island lifer, but he thought she was overdoing it. Also, he was pretty sure the glitter from the pattern on her comforter was giving him a rash.

"And why Checkmate again?" he asked.

"It's the quiet thing," said Hannah. "He never talks or makes any noise, so it's like you don't know he's coming up behind you until, bam, checkmate, you're done."

"Terrifying," he said. "Why's he hanging out with Derek?"

"That's just one of the many mysteries surrounding him. Because we all know hanging out with Derek is something the powers that be make you do after you die if you've been really bad."

Their laughter was interrupted by Hannah's dad, Gary, poking his head in to check on them. Alec noticed that he had dark, bruise-colored rings around his eyes, and blinked hard and constantly to keep himself awake and alert.

"We're going to put Joan down and then head for

bed ourselves," said Mr. Maplethorpe. "Lights out soon, though, okay? I can hear you cackling from across the house."

"We're just poking fun at Derek Rector," said Hannah.

"Oh man, his dad was the toughest guy in high school." Mr. Maplethorpe shook his head. "He had a bomber jacket with all nine of the dudes from Slipknot stitched into the back. It was nuts."

"Sounds legit," said Alec. After Mr. Maplethorpe wished them a final good night and left, Alec looked to Hannah with concern. "Everything okay with your pops? He looks tired."

"They're sleep-training Joan," she said. "Moving her from two naps a day to one, and trying to get her to sleep at night. Apparently, the blackouts are making everything difficult."

Alec nodded, the mention of the blackouts re-focusing him on the task at hand. He checked his phone—7:58. He got his pen and notebook laid out in front of him; since all their technology would be dead, this was the only way he could take notes, even if they were poorly written.

"You got the string?" he asked.

"Yeah," said Hannah, producing a ball of twine. "I'm glad you liked this idea, by the way."

"It's genius," said Alec, and he meant it. Hannah had talked about not wanting to go stumbling around in the dark, so she'd come up with the idea of tying strings to major points in her room so they could follow them from point A to point B. She had it organized by bedpost—top left was her dresser, top right was a basket they'd set up full of snacks and Cokes (they were going to try and stay up for the whole blackout). Bottom left was the window, and bottom right led to her door. (She'd originally suggested the idea of the final string going straight to the bathroom, but Alec had pictured Hannah's mom tripping over it and getting hurt, and maybe peeing herself in the process.)

They ran the strings from the posts to their assigned spots, careful to give each one enough slack so they wouldn't get clotheslined in the darkness. Then Alec went into his bag and found the book of matches he'd grabbed from Mom's dresser. He wanted to test the whole fire-but-no-light stories everyone had been telling, but they couldn't light a candle or anything—too risky to knock it over in the dark.

Finally, everything in place, Alec lay down on his sleeping bag next to Hannah's bed. His notebook ready, the matches in his pocket, there was only one thing left: to wait for the darkness.

They waited.

And waited.

"What time is it?" asked Hannah.

Alec checked his phone. "Eight thirty-one. Should be any minute now."

"I hate that they're random." Hannah sighed. "That makes it all the scarier. Having no idea when it's going to happen."

"Well, that's why we're doing this test, right?" said Alec. "Locking down a time frame."

Hannah groaned. "Maybe we should just leave it up to that long-haired dude at the meeting."

"I feel you. But for now, we have to be—"

The room went pitch-black around them.

"—patient."

"Whoa," whispered Hannah.

Alec pressed the home button on his phone—nothing. He found his pen and notebook and scribbled down, *Blackout commenced a little after 8:31.* He had no idea if his pen was making any sense on the paper—it was really hard to write when you couldn't see a thing.

"Guys, are you okay?" Mr. Maplethorpe asked from the hall. "I think we're in another blackout—"

"We're fine!" Hannah answered. "We'll stay put!"

"Holler if you need us," he said. Then they heard quiet footsteps and a closed door. Alec heard Hannah exhale sharply. They had planned for this—her mom and dad were so exhausted from dealing with Joan that they weren't going to play the hero and go stumbling around in the darkness just because they heard a little noise from Hannah's room. They'd be asleep in no time.

"Trying match test," said Alec. He ripped a match out of the book and scratched it against the stripe on the back. He heard the sulfur hiss, felt a bloom of heat—but there was no light. He waved the match in the air, the smell of smoke letting him know it was out. "Match ignites . . . but does not give off light," he muttered as he wrote.

"That's spooky," said Hannah. "It's like a black hole or something. Not even light can escape it."

Black hole? noted Alec before setting down his pen.

"Okay, next step," he said. "Let's go to the window."

They found the string attached to Hannah's bottom-left bedpost and followed it to the window, moving hand over hand like climbers ascending a mountain. Even with the help of the rope, they managed to make a lot of noise and nearly trip over Hannah's backpack and die, but eventually they reached the window and pushed it open.

"*Super* spooky," whispered Hannah, and Alec agreed. Outside Hannah's window, the night was darker than dark, complete and total in its blackness. They could still hear the noises of the island outside— the crash of waves on rocks, the hum of a generator or two—but in the complete nothingness, it felt like whatever was making them could be a million miles away.

"Any sign of those creatures, like the one in the basement?" asked Hannah.

"None yet," said Alec. "But keep your ears peeled."

They sat in the fathomless darkness for a few

minutes—and then they heard the howling off in the distance, melancholy and bloodcurdling. Just like before, the first howl was met with another, then another. The closest they heard was a few houses away, and when it sounded, the others responded swiftly.

"They're communicating," whispered Alec. "The one nearby obviously said something important, because the others were quick to respond."

"What are they looking for?" asked Hannah.

"Maybe each other . . . or prey," said Alec. He flashed back to their day in the school basement, to the door bucking against his shoulder as that *thing* threw itself against it, and his mouth went dry. He felt Hannah shudder next to him and wondered if she was reliving the same memory.

They listened for a few more minutes, but heard no more—either the creatures were done talking, or they weren't conversing across the island. After a while, Alec patted Hannah's shoulder and said, "Let's close the window. I'll make notes and we can chug some soda. It's going to be a long night."

"Good call," whispered Hannah. Alec reached for the

edge of the window and started to pull down—and then Hannah said at full volume, "Whoa, what's *THAT*?"

"Shhh!" hissed Alec, jumping and grabbing her bicep. Hannah's voice might as well have been a gunshot in the blackout. He could've sworn that he'd heard one of those things start moving around down in the grass the minute she'd spoken. "What's *what*?"

"That green thing on the fence," she said.

Alec looked down at the lawn—and felt a surge of confusion, excitement, and horror all at once.

On the fence at the edge of the Honeycomb's backyard was a green spot that glowed out of the night.

Alec's mind raced. "I have no clue," he said. "Could it be some kind of glowing bug? Or, like, a luminescent moss?"

"Well, obviously it's gotta be a *luminescent moss*," said Hannah. "Wait, let me try something."

Hannah shifted next to Alec—and suddenly, the green mark was right in front of them, a bean-shaped spot on Hannah's palm.

"It's light," she said. She shifted, looking up, and then whispered, "Alec, look. Third floor."

Alec twisted and looked up. On the third floor of the Honeycomb was a window, completely blacked out with paint—except for a small hole in the covering, out of which spilled the green light.

"Whatever it is," said Hannah, "it's coming from inside my house."

9

THE GLOW

They crept stealthily back to the bed and then along the string to the door. Outside Hannah's room, the Honeycomb felt as massive and threatening as outer space. Hannah and Alec shuffled forward, with one of Alec's hands against the wall and the other against Hannah's back, until they reached a staircase.

"Look," whispered Hannah. "There's more light."

Almost instantly, Alec saw a change in the lighting of the house—though barely perceptible, he could *just* make out the shapes of the stairs leading up to the third floor, each one more and more outlined with a bright, radioactive green.

They climbed up to the landing, only to discover that the stairs got still greener as they went up farther, to what Hannah whispered was "the attic floor."

"What's up there?" asked Alec.

"Just attic space and one or two old empty rooms no one uses," she responded. "Be careful, these stairs aren't as new as the others."

She wasn't joking—with every step, a new round of creaks and groans filled the house around them. But finally, they came to another landing, and stood before a door outlined in green light so bright that even the glow spilling out from the edges seemed to burn brighter than anything Alec had ever seen. Then again, he thought, maybe it was just the blackout around them making any light seem especially powerful.

"What do we do?" asked Alec, staring at the green rectangle in the darkness before him.

"I don't know," admitted Hannah. "I have no clue—"

"*Hannah.*"

They both jumped and gasped. The voice had come from behind the door, not loud but firm and calm.

A voice, Alec realized, that he knew.

"Hannah, you and your friend come on in," it said. *"Just be quiet."*

Hannah stepped forward and took the knob. Alec was gripped by a moment of sheer, unexplainable terror, and said, "Hannah, wait."

Hannah yanked the door open and filled the hallway with blazing green light.

The room was huge and empty, its triangular ceiling lit a brilliant lime green. At the far end, near the painted-over window, Big Gran sat in an overstuffed armchair. At her feet a little ways away was an old wooden cradle, which she gently rocked with one big toe. As Alec and Hannah approached, they saw that Joan, Hannah's new sister, lay there in a swaddle of blankets, her tiny hands folded just below her chin as though she were a chubby-cheeked little Dracula.

"Big Gran, what are you doing up here?" asked Hannah.

"Lower your voice, child," said Big Gran in that same low, steady tone. "The baby needs to sleep. She wouldn't be getting much of it, if all of you idiots had your way. As long as she sleeps, it's my job to protect her."

"Where's all the light coming from?" asked Alec.

"This," said Gran. She reached up to her neck, holding up a smooth rock at the end of a small hemp rope. This close, the stone burned green so bright that Alec worried it might be hot to the touch, and yet Gran held it aloft without any sign of pain.

Alec had a million questions. He wanted to hear everything Big Gran had to tell them, about where the glowing rock had come from. But something dawned on him—something he couldn't pass up.

"Before we go any further," he said, "let me point out an important fact." He looked at Hannah, raised an eyebrow, and gestured to Big Gran's necklace. Hannah stared for a moment, confused—and then her shoulders fell with a huff.

"It's a *rock*," she said. "Oh God, the answer *was* geology! How pleased are *you*, Alec?"

"Dorky hobbies, *one*," said Alec. "Being a normal kid, *zero*."

Big Gran shook her head. "Kids today. You two sit

down. You, boy, take over rocking that cradle. I gotta collect myself if I want to get this right."

As Hannah and Alec sat down at her feet, Big Gran stared off into the distance with her one good eye, and started talking, low and fast . . .

10

THE SLEEPER

Thing you gotta remember is that Founders has always been strange. Down-to-the-bone strange, Bermuda Triangle strange. We got animals here that don't show up anywhere else. We got rocks that aren't rocks—yeah, I see you, kid. Plenty of rocks here for you to look at, if you need to make sure you never have a date.

("Hey!" said Alec.)

And we also got the blackouts. From what I can

tell, they happen once every couple of decades, sometimes nearly a century. I'm the only person here who's still alive after the last ones. I remember it all perfectly, though. I was five, barely able to read or write, but kids were older in those days. They grew up faster. By that age, my mother was already handing me the baby and sending me down to the store. I was on my way to the drugstore downtown, sent to get some medicine for my sister. There was some change, so I got a scoop of ice cream with coconut. I had just finished when the whole world went dark.

("I thought you said you were at a pharmacy," said Hannah.

"It was a *drugstore*," said Big Gran. "They also sold loose candy and ice cream at drugstores then."

"That sounds unsanitary," said Alec.

"You're going to wake the baby," said Big Gran. "Hush and listen.")

The first one was bad, but then they started happening more often, for different amounts of time. There were fewer people on the island then, but it was still awful—everyone carrying on, people running in the streets in the dark. A lot of folks thought it was judgment from on high or a Martian invasion or one of those things that was just too easy to be real. My mother worried that it was some sort of war threat, that some nation was using a chemical weapon on us like they had in the Great War. She started making me go down to the basement of this house to be safe.

It was down there that I found this stone. Just a teeny-tiny bit of green light shining out of a crack in the concrete. Next time I was down there, I brought a screwdriver with me and dug it out. Back then it glowed even brighter than this, if you can believe it. I kept it from my parents, mostly just because I knew they'd be foolish and use it outside, or try to help out the town. They were sweet people, mind you, but simple. Me, I knew the story about the goose that laid the golden eggs. I knew the townsfolk would end up using it wrong or destroying it.

("What happened to the goose that laid the golden eggs?" asked Alec.

Hannah looked over at him funny. "The townsfolk ripped it open to try and get all the eggs at once. But they killed it, so there were no more golden eggs."

"Oh," said Alec. "Huh."

"Did you really not know the goose that laid the golden eggs?" she asked.

"I didn't grow up on some fisherman's island hearing tales around a campfire," said Alec.

"That's a standard-issue fairy tale, dude," said Hannah. "That one's not regional. *Everyone* knows that story."

"Children, please," sighed Big Gran.)

I hid it. Used it only late at night, when my parents and everyone else in town were dead asleep. The light helped me get around, keep things in order, and scare off those scrabblers.

Oh, yes, they were there, too. Horrible things, creeping through yards, calling to each other at night, eating local cats like they were hotcakes. They don't like the light, mind, maybe because it lets you see how ugly they really are. I don't want to give you kids nightmares, but take it from me, they ain't pretty.

I also learned it wasn't just me. One night, while scaring off a big scrabbler trying to come down through our chimney, I looked out my window and saw another green light in the distance. Started using mine to flash messages to the other, and eventually we met up. Turned out to be my school friend Bobby. When he showed me his stone, it was obvious that ours were two halves of the same piece. And when we put it together, it had a sort of a vibration. Made the comet light up overhead, too. And it guided us to the sleeper, the one causing all this trouble.

Only once that happened, things changed. Those scrabblers started following us—they weren't afraid anymore. They loved the light. And Bobby said he heard other things out in the dark, voices telling him to bring them the sleeper and the stone. He even said he heard them after this all had passed and the black-outs stopped. Anyway, we broke the stone back in half, and promised to hide the pieces.

That's why I only have half. And maybe that's better. This time, I knew the sleeper from the start. And this way, I can protect her without drawing attention.

"Her?" said Hannah.

Big Gran glanced at her watch and nodded. "Well, you had to learn eventually. And anyway, she ate poorly before bed, so she could do with a feeding. Hand me your sister."

Alec's and Hannah's eyes fell on Joan, snug in the cradle beside them. Gently, Hannah reached in and lifted the baby out, a tail of blanket dragging after her little body. Joan squirmed and made a face like she'd smelled something terrible, but otherwise stayed perfectly asleep.

"Deep sleeper, this one," mumbled Big Gran, taking the baby from Hannah and producing a bottle from beside the armchair. She nudged Joan's upper lip with the nipple of the bottle and softly said, "Hey, there, little miss. Hey there, sweet darling. You hungry? Want a little midnight snack?"

Joan squirmed, grunted, and slowly opened her eyes.

The bare bulb in the room's ceiling was on in a flash. Hannah and Alec squinted against the harsh light—and then realized what it meant. They checked their phones and saw their lock screens glowing back at them. The green rock hung limp and tarnished from Big Gran's neck, not even glowing.

Alec felt a surge of excitement as the realization exploded in his head. He shared a stunned glance with

Hannah and then stared in awe at the tiny bundle sucking at the bottle held in Big Gran's leathery old hands.

"Joan?" asked Hannah.

Big Gran nodded. "When she sleeps," said the old woman, "everything goes black."

11

ROCKABYE, BABY

"We are not giving my infant sister caffeine," snapped Hannah.

"Look, I'm not saying it's the perfect option," said Alec, "or our first line of defense. But a little Coke in the bottle—"

"No buts," said Hannah firmly. "You'll stunt her growth or something. We need to come up with a better option than *jack the baby up on soda pop.*"

Alec sighed and looked for an idea in the overcast

sky. He and Hannah sat on the Honeycomb's front porch, picking at the breakfast her mom had made them. They were trying to come up with ways to fix the island's blackout problem—without harming Hannah's innocent baby sister. Alec's first instinct was that if the town wanted to keep the blackouts at bay, they should just sort of . . . keep Joan awake. But the more he talked to Hannah about it, the more he realized that this wasn't really possible. Babies slept whether you wanted them to or not, and forcing one not to sleep was basically torture. At least with the sleep training, Joan was just down to one nap and nighttime.

His other idea had been to tell Hannah's parents, but Big Gran made them swear to silence. "You know your mom, Hannah," she'd said, and Hannah had nodded and wouldn't consider the idea from then on. Alec kind of understood—Hannah's mother, Jackie, was one of those moms who insisted on confronting every issue with her sleeves rolled up. The story around his class was that when Hannah got detention for giving a presentation at school that totally slammed Christopher Columbus, Jackie showed up with three representatives from mainland Native activist groups to protest the punishment. If she found out Joan was causing the blackouts, there'd be doctors and psychologists, and eventually the whole town would know what was going on.

"And then she'd be in danger," Big Gran had said.

"From who?" asked Alec.

"Come on, boy," Big Gran spat. "Who do you think those creepy crawlers out there are looking for?"

Thinking of one of those strange, howling scrabblers lowering itself over Joan's crib made Alec cringe with disgust. He didn't even know what they looked like, but he somehow knew that whatever they wanted, it was wrong.

They had to keep Joan safe from the scrabblers.

Which left them with very few options.

"We have to talk to Derek," Hannah said through a mouthful of Golden Grahams. "It's our only option. The guy Big Gran called Bobby—that's Robert Rector, Derek's ancestor. She's mentioned him before."

"We already know it's your sister causing the blackouts," argued Alec. "We don't need the two stones if they're not going to lead us to anything."

"Two stones are better than one," said Hannah,

"and uniting them might move things along. You heard what Gran said—together, they made the comet light up, and things got better afterward. This might be our chance."

"There's got to be another way," said Alec, pushing his mind as far as it would go. He wanted to do anything *but* talk to Derek. But he couldn't deny that Hannah had a point—the blackouts eventually stopped once Big Gran found the other half of the stone, even if it had taken a strange turn. But still . . . *Derek*.

"Ugh, I wish I could think of something else," he groaned. "My dad would've been able to come up with something. He was always such a good strategist. That's why he was so successful at his job."

"Yeah, well," said Hannah, "since he isn't here, it looks like talking to Derek is what we're working with."

"Great, so to unravel the mystery of the blackouts, I have to sit there and listen to insults from a total cretin."

Hannah nodded. "Nobody said this would be fun, dude."

It was a lead. It was part of the bigger story of the

blackouts. To ignore it because Derek was a jerk was to admit that he cared about himself more than saving the whole island.

"All right, we'll reach out to him," said Alec. "But if he starts being a complete dingus right from the start, I'm out of there."

"Oh, good, this is exactly how I wanted to spend my day," said Derek, "annoyed by some scrawny mainland hippie teacher's son. Good times."

Alec stopped and clenched his teeth tight. Hannah put her hand on his lower back and pushed him forward, whispering, "You knew this would happen. Come on."

Derek shot Alec the stink eye from his lawn, where he and Checkmate were running a long rope between his front porch and a stake buried out in the yard. Hanging from the rope were various pieces of metal—old cans, bunches of keys, what looked like a few decrepit wind chimes. All of them were red and scabby with rust; the Rectors' big, old colonial house was down near the boardwalk, and Alec could taste heavy doses of salt water on the breeze.

"What's this?" asked Hannah, gesturing to the rope.

Derek's scowl softened a touch. "Warning device," he said. "We figured this'd let us know if one of those big . . . *things* is moving around the yard."

"Not a bad idea," she said.

"Thanks," said Derek. He put his hands on his hips and surveyed his handiwork. "A little primitive, but, you know, desperate times. Right, Checkmate?" From the porch, Checkmate gave a large thumbs-up.

"We have to talk to you about something," said Alec.

"Whatever it is, you can figure it out for yourself, newbie," said Derek. "I'm not here to hold your hand just because you moved to this island when things got rough—"

"We think we're onto something," said Hannah. "A way to stop the blackouts. Or at least get through them unscathed."

Derek raised his eyebrows. "Really. That I'd like to hear. What'd you find out?"

Hannah opened her mouth to answer, but Alec decided it was now or never.

"First things first, I'm done with the constant insults," he said. "I don't care how long your family's lived here and mine hasn't. If you want to hear what we have to tell you, just leave me alone. Got it?"

Derek eyed Alec coolly, like he was choosing between accepting the offer or punching him in the nose. He glanced over his shoulder at Checkmate; the big, silent boy shrugged, then nodded.

"Fine," Derek sighed, like it was a huge hassle. "But this better be good."

They sat on the front steps of the house, and Hannah and Alec recounted Big Gran's story as best they could. Derek made disbelieving faces the whole time, but he stayed silent as Hannah told the tale of his great-grandfather and Big Gran finding the stones. Hannah made a point of leaving out baby Joan.

"So you, what, came here looking for the other half of this chunk of green rock?" asked Derek when they were done. "No offense, Hannah, but I don't know if I buy it. Your grandma's, what, a hundred and five? She could have just been remembering something she saw in a movie once."

"We saw the rock, Derek," she said. "It lit up the whole room. If your great-grandfather hid the other half somewhere, and we find it, we can—"

"What?" he asked. "What happens when we put the BFF necklace back together?"

"We're not exactly sure," said Hannah. "Gran said it caused a sort of vibration that made the scrabblers calm down and follow her around. And it seemed to guide them toward whatever was causing the blackouts." She glanced at Alec, then at the floor. "They never found out what that was, of course."

Derek considered this, then looked at Alec. "You believe all this magic, science boy? Sounds like the kind of stuff you'd pick holes in until it fell apart."

"I saw the rock, too," said Alec. "It all checks out."

"Well, that's your answer, then." Derek took out his phone. "It's, what, almost eleven right now. If we book it back to your place, Maplethorpe, and if the blackout happens around the same time it's happened before, we can get there just in time to see this thing in action. Then, if you're for real, you can start going through my family's house."

Alec got ready to say no deal, but this time Hannah cut him off.

"You don't have to," she said. She reached into her pocket and pulled out the green stone. It looked ordinary, even a little dingy, in the gray light. Alec held his tongue, but inside, he couldn't believe that Hannah had brought it here.

Derek whistled. "There you go. Gran know you took her precious heirloom?"

Alec waited to hear Hannah explain that, yes, she'd only borrowed it, but instead she just screwed up her mouth and said, "Let's get inside. I have a feeling it'll be dark soon."

Derek's room smelled exactly like Alec had imagined it would: rotten sweat, greasy food, and maybe a dash of fungus. The walls were plastered with pictures of military ships and famous soccer players, and the floor was dotted with piles of old laundry that Alec had to tiptoe around to find a good seat. Of course, Derek was quick to clear a spot on his bed for Hannah, going so far as to smooth the sheets.

"My mom and dad are closing down the rental office, and my sister's riding things out at Shirley Clanahan's tonight," he explained solely to Hannah. "So we have the whole place to ourselves."

"Uh . . . great," she replied uneasily.

While he wasn't exactly overjoyed that Hannah

had swiped Big Gran's magic glowing stone—"She'll understand," had been Hannah's whispered response to Alec's questioning, though her expression said that it might not be so simple—this did give Alec a moment to observe the stone up close. For a kid who loved rocks, getting to examine some sort of paranormal gem was like a birthday and Christmas rolled into one.

The only problem was, the more he turned the rock over in his hands, the less he knew. The stone wasn't like anything he'd ever seen or read about, neither igneous nor sedimentary nor metamorphic. It didn't feel like a precious gem or volcanic glass, either; the outside had an opaque layer to it, while the broken, jagged part on its side showed a gleaming, gem-like interior. It had no pores, and yet it felt almost soft in his hands, as though with enough pressure it might squish rather than break. For some reason, Alec kept thinking of stale gummy bears while holding it.

He felt a presence at his side, like someone watching him, and this time he recognized the sensation. Sure enough, a long, pale face was bent near his, watching the rock with cold, intense eyes.

"I . . . I've never seen anything like this before," he told Checkmate, holding up the rock. "See, geology's my hobby, so I should be able to identify this. But I think it's completely new. This might be a huge scientific discovery, if we were to show it to someone."

"Hmm," said Checkmate, rubbing his lips with a knuckle. It was the most noise Alec had ever heard the guy make.

"Let's get ready, folks. Blackout could start any minute," said Derek. He turned to Hannah. "You need anything? Juice? Spindrift?"

"I'm good," said Hannah.

Alec's teeth buzzed. "Hey, guys," he said.

"My folks got Spindrift," said Derek. "Ice cold. Really tasty—"

Darkness fell, cutting Derek off. Everyone gasped.

As always with the dark, Alec felt the sudden rush of his other senses, with the stench of Derek's filthy clothes closing in around him, so heavy that he thought he might puke . . .

And then the green light rose out of the stone.

"Look," said Alec, watching in awe. The glow

started as a pinprick deep in the rock's core, flickering like candlelight. Then it stretched and twisted, growing bigger and bigger with each pulse, until it finally filled the entire rock and bathed the whole room in steady green light. Again, Alec was worried something so bright might burn him, but the stone remained cool in his palm.

Hannah, Derek, and Checkmate all crowded around him, softly cooing over the light that spilled out of the stone.

"Man, you weren't lying," said Derek. "Dude, if we found a way to set this up with some mirrors, like a lighthouse? We could light the whole town."

"We're not sure that's a good idea," said Hannah. "Big Gran was worried that the townsfolk would misuse it."

"Yeah, like the turkey who pooped gold coins or whatever," said Alec.

"Actually, knowing the people around here, that makes sense," said Derek. He glanced at Alec. "You mean the goose, right? With the golden eggs? Do you really not know—"

The sound of jangling metal yanked all their heads

up. Outside of Derek's window, a racket of clinking and clanging filled the air . . . along with a series of grunts and strange snarling noises.

"We got one," said Derek. He looked back at the stone with a sharp smile on his face. "Big Gran said this would scare them off, right?"

12

THE SCRABBLER

They crept downstairs through Derek's house, Hannah taking the lead with the stone held out in front of her like a torch. In the green light, Alec thought Derek's place looked especially haunted, the stuffed game fish and pictures of old ships on the walls throwing long, weird shadows that looked like portals into the blackout.

Just before they go to the door, Hannah froze and lowered the rock. "Wait. We can't go out there like this."

"Why not?" asked Derek.

"If we go out with the rock, everyone in town will see it from their windows," she said. "They'll come running here, looking for the light. It'll be chaos."

Derek looked frustrated for a moment—and then he snapped his fingers. "Come with me," he said, and led them to the kitchen. He riffled around in a cabinet drawer until he found an old flashlight. Then he took the head off, dumped out the batteries, and popped the lens off the guts. Sure enough, the rock fit into the shaft of the flashlight, and when Derek screwed the lens back on, it created a perfect beam of green light.

"We keep it aimed low," he said. "That way, it's contained. People might see it, but not as many."

"That's pretty smart," said Alec.

"You learn a lot of useless stuff on boats," he said. "Come on."

They headed out front by the glow of the flashlight. Outside, the world still felt vast and empty to Alec, but having the beam of light automatically made things a little less scary and put the crashing sounds around him in perspective rather than making him feel like they were all on top of him.

He could feel Derek's porch vibrating beneath them, though. And a quick flicker for the flashlight showed the rope tied to one post shaking wildly. Out on the lawn, they could hear the clattering of metal even louder now, along with wet grunts and steady, frantic clicking that vibrated deep in Alec's inner ear.

The four of them stood perfectly still, flashlight pinned on the thrashing end of the rope.

"Well, let's go see what it looks like," said Derek, his voice cracking slightly.

"Okay," said Alec, feeling his heart pounding in his chest. "Let's do it."

None of them moved.

"Now," said Hannah. Finally, the group moved forward in a single, huddled blob. They got to the edge of the porch, and Derek moved the flashlight down the shaking rope, closer and closer to the source of the horrible sound. As it got nearer, Alec saw two eyes glitter out of the darkness, like those of a cat. As the light reached the first of its spindly black limbs, the thing recoiled and released a fresh set of panicked clicks.

It's a giant cave cricket, thought Alec. He wasn't far off: The thing was about the size of a deer, and mostly made up of long, arched legs that jutted out of its bulbous body. Its back end was large and hunched, bending like the tail of a wasp, only instead of a stinger, there was only some sort of opening in its shiny exoskeleton that leaked a thick, dark goo. Up by its head was a set of arms stretched out before it, each ending in a hand with two long, spindly fingers. But most horrible was that it had the head of a corpse—or more that it wore a corpse's face as a mask, with the pale, rotting skin of a human stretched over its head, the lower jaw hanging limp from its chin so that the thing seemed to be perpetually screaming. But all that meant was that when the light hit its face, it was a white, bloated *human* face that stared back at them, a human brow that creased angrily over glittering black eyes, and a human mouth out of which the thing emitted a hideous shriek of pain.

Alec felt himself gag; he hunched his shoulders as a wave of disgust moved over him and he wondered if he might faint. Derek's hand shook, making the beam of the light dance over the monster's face. Hannah just kept saying "Oh God" over and over again. Checkmate calmly walked to the other side of the porch and leaned over the edge, and Alec heard him puke long and hard.

"*Look* at it," said Derek hoarsely. "We . . . we gotta kill it. We gotta get rid of it."

Alec pushed through his horror to make his numb lips move. "I don't think it's dangerous," he mumbled. As he watched the scrabbler cower and click, he realized that it wasn't attacking them—more than that, it was *scared* of them. The creature's legs seized up around its body, and it frantically tried to cover its face with its skinny fingers. It hated the light, and would have fled from them if not for the rope tangled around the legs on its right side.

Checkmate rejoined them, wiping his mouth. Together, they stared at the writhing, whimpering scrabbler in silent awe as it tried to shield its eyes from the green beam and get itself loose from the rope.

"Should we help it?" asked Hannah.

"Are you kidding me?" asked Derek. "I'm not getting anywhere near that thing. It'll disappear when the blackout's over."

Alec hadn't even thought of that, but he realized Derek was right. The things just *didn't exist* when Joan was awake. How did *that* work? Would the scrabbler appear back here, tangled up in the ropes, when Hannah's sister went to sleep tonight?

A flicker of inquisitiveness ran through Alec. Barely thinking, he snatched the flashlight out of Derek's hand and trotted down the porch steps, ignoring Derek's angry cry and Hannah calling his name. He didn't know if it was his scientific curiosity pushing him forward, or maybe just some need to look this horrible thing right in the face, but even though he was grossed out, he couldn't stop himself.

The closer he got, the more the scrabbler twisted away from the light and tried to hide itself. But the harder it fought, the more it got tangled in Derek's simple trap and only succeeded in making more noise. It kept darting its abdomen toward Alec and releasing more of the thick goop dripping from it, but in its tangled state it looked like the stuff was just piling up under its legs and making it slip when it tried to run.

Something on the creature's cheek caught Alec's eye. He peered closer, trying to ignore the hideous mandibles moving beneath the dead skin mask of its face.

"It has a tattoo," he said.

"What?" called Hannah.

"A tattoo of a key," he said. "Under its left eye."

"Alec, will you please just get back here—"

The scrabbler stopped its frantic pulling at the rope and raised its head to the sky. It let out the long, warbling howl that he'd heard those nights before, making the dangling lower jaw of its human mask quiver repulsively.

Alec felt static prickle up the back of his neck as another howl answered this one . . .

Only a few feet behind him.

He wheeled, and the beam of the flashlight caught another scrabbler scuttling toward him, this one wearing the long-dead face of a woman. The thing reared up and screeched in pain as the light hit it.

For a split second, Alec saw its huge abdomen curl between its legs—and then a gob of thick gray goo fired from its tail end and hit Alec right in the hand.

Covering the front of the flashlight.

Alec cried out as the light dropped down to a faint glimmer. He pawed at the warm slime all over his hand, but now he was the one getting even further caught the more he struggled. Each time he touched the stuff, it stuck to his skin more and more, making his hands a webbed mess of gray snot. He began to hyperventilate, his panic rising, his breathing getting faster and faster—

He heard a long string of clicks and looked up to see eyes glittering in the faint glow from the flashlight. They hung a foot from his face, so close that Alec could smell its rotten breath . . .

WHAM!—a shape launched out of the dark and threw its shoulder into the scrabbler's head. At the same time, hands closed around Alec's arms and yanked him backward across the lawn, up the stairs, and through the door of Derek's house. No sooner were they inside than Checkmate leapt in behind them, slammed the door, and threw the lock.

"Come on," said Derek. He and Hannah led Alec by the flashlight back to the kitchen. They put his goo-covered hands under a hot tap, and with a heavy squirt of dish soap, they managed to wash off most of the stuff, until they could pop the flashlight back open and retrieve the rock from inside. Once more, the room was a brilliant green, everyone's brows sparkling with sweat in the light from the stone.

"That was close," said Alec. He caught his breath for a moment and realized what had happened. "Thank you for saving me, guys. I don't know what they would've done if those things had gotten ahold of me."

"No problem," said Derek. "What *were* they, anyway? Could you tell, up close? Are those bugs, or . . . people?"

"Sort of both," said Alec, his mind racing with fear.

"You said one had a tattoo on its face?" asked Hannah.

"Yeah," said Alec. Then, slowly, as the fireworks in his brain began to fade away, a memory came to him. A memory of the second scrabbler that he'd seen for only a second in the flashlight's beam.

"Actually," he said, "they both did. Under the same eye."

13

LOCKED AWAY

"It's all up here," said Derek's mom, Janice, twisting the knob and letting the door swing inward with a creak. Behind it loomed an attic space, gray with dust.

"Thanks, Ma," said Derek. "I promise, we'll put everything back the way we found it."

"All right, honey," she said, and then took Derek's face in her hands again and peered at him. "You sure you're okay? You look a little pale. Did anything happen during the blackout?"

"I'm fine, Ma," he said, brushing her away. Alec had to bite the inside of his cheek to keep from shouting out, *WE FOUGHT A GIANT BUG THAT LIVES INSIDE OF THE BLACKOUT.* He remembered Big Gran's warning about the stone—*sweet people, but real simple.* That was grown-ups all over, trying to make things better but only tripping over their own feet and refusing to believe their eyes.

The attic smelled like sour wood and old paper, lit faintly by sunlight coming in through a circular window at one end. Stacks of boxes, racks of old clothes, and piles of renovation materials were shoved under the slanted ceiling and left to congeal. Derek led the way, picking up an old umbrella near the door and machete-ing a path through the endless spiderwebs that filled the space. Alec felt one glance across his face and couldn't even be bothered to shiver. After what they'd been through that morning, a little spider wasn't going to faze him.

"Remember, we're looking for a trunk," said Derek. "Old, green, probably got my grandfather's initials on it. 'GR.'"

"Wouldn't Robert Rector be 'RR'?" asked Alec.

"That's my *great*-grandad," said Derek. "Grampa's the one who kept all the family tree stuff. Get a legacy, newbie."

Alec ignored the cheap shot and started poking around between moldy coats and dusty boxes. Derek was a jerk, but he had to admit, there was something about his and Hannah's old houses that he envied. His mom was originally from Indiana and didn't much care to go back—she'd had a bad relationship with her family—while Dad had grown up in a tiny apartment in the Chinatown part of San Francisco. Alec's home growing up had been clean and neat, but it didn't have the memories and background an old house like this had. It was an odd feeling, he thought, missing something he'd never had.

He shoved aside a stack of boxes, scanning them for any markings that would indicate they contained Derek's family history. All he saw were black Sharpie scribblings of CHRISTMAS DECORATIONS, OLD METAL MAGAZINES, CLOTHES—BABY DEREK . . .

A muffled noise rose up from the floorboards, and Alec froze. He knew it perfectly—a mom and a dad shouting at each other across a bedroom. Déjà vu hit him, and suddenly he was back in his old room in San Francisco again, ear plastered to the wall, trying to make out what his parents were screaming at each other. He glanced up at Derek, who was arms-deep in a box full of what looked to be old sheets.

"Just ignore it," mumbled Derek, not even looking up at him. "Usually doesn't go more than a couple of minutes."

Alec thought back on his own parents' fighting, and tried to think of something to say. Finally, he came up with: "Who leaves?"

Derek paused and stared into the box for a moment. "Mom," he said. "She goes *power-walking*."

"My dad said he was going out with friends," said Alec. He swallowed hard. He felt sick and awkward even saying it, but the opportunity to talk about it felt compelling. It was like when he'd taken the flashlight earlier that day—something he didn't like doing but felt he couldn't stop himself from. "But I think now that he was going over to someone else's house."

Derek nodded slowly and arched an eyebrow. "Sucks," he said, and went back to his digging. Alec nodded and mumbled, "Yeah," before returning to his own search. He didn't know what he'd expected from Derek, but he was glad he'd said something.

A few minutes later, Checkmate whistled, then dragged a wooden trunk out from the center of a pile of boxes. The thing was older than any of them, the green paint on its wooden surfaces flaking, the nailed metal panels holding it all together rusty and old. A large, flat mushroom was growing out of one side in thick, shelflike panels. On the front, above the latch, was a tarnished metal panel with the letters *GR* on it.

"Bingo," said Derek. He threw the top open with a bang and a cloud of dust motes. Inside were stacks of old boxes, thick folders, and a couple of books. Slowly, Derek passed them out for the four of them to look through, muttering, "Be careful," as he handed a stack of books to Alec.

Most of what they paged through were old photos of Derek's grandfather and grandmother, with the occasional picture of Derek's dad, Herman, as a toddler. The books were full of newspaper clippings, receipts, and old tax documents, and the boxes were packed with pure junk like passports with holes in them and change in foreign coins. Alec's hands were covered with dust, and he was just about ready to suggest they keep looking elsewhere when Hannah said, "I found something."

It was a small black notebook, filled with thin, ragtag script—Robert Rector's diary, according to the way the entries were dated. Hannah flipped through the pages while the three boys crowded around her, peering at the scrawled handwriting in the hopes that it'd reveal something to them.

"I can't even read this chicken scratch," said Alec. "Are you having any luck, Hannah?"

"A little," she said. "But honestly, it's mostly boring. Look—'*Tried eggs over hard today, have to say I don't like it . . . Went out to Founders Gulch, looked for frogs with Martin and the boys . . . They say it'll storm this week, got to board up the basement . . .*'" She shrugged. "Sorry, guys, this might just be some old man's diary."

She flipped a page.

In huge, splotchy letters, it read, *THE DARKNESS IS GONE, BUT HE IS STILL HERE.*

"Ah," said Hannah. "Never mind, then."

She turned to the next page, and it was as though the diary had been handed from a polite schoolboy to an overcaffeinated beast. The script was now wild and smeared, cutting in weird diagonals across the page. Included with it were drawings—scribbled depictions of eyes in the dark, many-legged creatures, and a black silhouette with its hand out. A recurring theme was repeated drawings of the outline of Founders Island, but usually with darkness dripping from it or long black veins coming of it.

"Now it's getting serious," said Hannah. "Listen: '*Somehow, I know the darkness is not gone. It exists beneath the island, beneath the Founders we all know. And in it, the First Man still dwells, leading his army. Even if we cannot see him . . .*'"

She turned the page. Pasted in the diary was an old picture, ripped out of a book by the looks of the edges. It was a portrait of a man in nineteenth-century garb, his coat plain and black. He had one hand outstretched, resting on a human skull and holding a black iron key. But where his face should have been beneath his wide-brimmed hat, Robert Rector had blacked it out furiously, and written over it in jagged lines, *DO NOT TRUST HIM.*

"Guess the blackouts got into his head," said Derek. "Didn't your grandmother say they started hearing voices? Maybe he cracked a little as he got older and kept hearing them."

"Any word about the other green rock?" asked Alec.

"No—wait, here," said Hannah. "'*I hope that Henrietta has gotten rid of her half of the summoning stone. Though it was useful to us in illuminating the darkness, I worry it could be dangerous if it fell into the wrong hands. Thankfully, mine will forever be safe in the shadow of the Cathedral.*'" Hannah lowered the book, and they all digested the entry for a moment.

"I didn't know Big Gran's name was Henrietta," said Alec.

"The cathedral," said Hannah softly. "It must be St. Brendan's, right? It's the only church on the island."

Checkmate reached out a long finger and tapped the word *Cathedral* in the journal. Alec stared at where he was pointing . . . and the truth flickered up in him like a flame on a match.

"It's *Cathedral* with a capital C," he said. "It's not a church, it's a place. The other half of the stone is hidden somewhere around Cathedral Rock."

14

TROUBLED WATER

Alec was halfway up the stairs when he heard Mom calling him. He slowed at the tone of her voice—high and distressed, definitely the way she sounded when she'd recently been crying. Part of him just wanted to pretend he didn't hear her, head up to his room, avoid whatever new drama was coming his way . . . but he couldn't just walk away from his mother. Not when she sounded like that.

He found her at the kitchen table, propping up her

head with her hand, her phone sitting in front of her. When she saw him, she gestured to one of the other chairs. After he sat, she stayed quiet for too long; the tension in the room was killing him, and he wondered how bad things could have possible gotten.

"Did you and Hannah have a good study session last night?" she asked. "Her parents are so nice for having you over so often. Let her know that she's always welcome to crash here."

"Yeah, it was fine," he said. *I was almost killed by a giant cricket monster*, he wanted to say, but figured that wouldn't be productive. Besides, there was obviously something else she wanted to talk about. "Everything okay, Mom?"

"It looks like things are taking a turn for the worse," she said. "People are seeing green lights moving around the countryside, and a lot of folks are panicking." She cleared her throat. "Most importantly, the mayor is ending incoming ferry service. Officially. The island will be isolated until these phenomena have stopped. She's encouraging locals to evacuate if they have family on the mainland."

"Whoa," said Alec. It was extreme, he knew, but

it also made sense. How many groups of tourists was this island expected to terrify before somebody made a decision?

"Yeah." She nodded. "And I've thought about it, and I'd like you to be on the last one out tomorrow."

"Sorry, what?" said Alec. He was stunned. That couldn't have been right. "You want me to leave?"

"I'm just not sure this place is safe for you right now, honey," said Mom. "With everything that's going on. I figured I would stay here, to deal with the house and other things. But with school canceled, and the blackouts still happening . . ."

Alec blinked, numb with disbelief. How was this happening now? It felt like she was yanking a rug out from under him. He'd spent all day elbow-deep in mystery and fringe science and giant bug monsters . . . and now he was supposed to just return to the mainland, where everything was normal?

"Where would I be going?" he asked. "Who'd I be living with?"

Mom took a long, deep breath, and exhaled sharply. "So, I just got off the phone with your father, and he was saying he could take you for at least a couple of weeks."

"You're sending me to stay with *Dad*? After what happened?"

Mom bit her lower lip. Her eyes glimmered with tears. "I know how much you miss him, honey. And that's okay. It's not something you have to hide from me—"

"What if I don't want to go back?" he asked.

"I'm sorry, kiddo," she said, "I never should have brought you here. Your dad, and his—and Suzanne, they're willing to take you until everything blows over. And by then, I'll be able—"

"Why don't I ever get a say in where I'm supposed to be?" he asked. It came out louder than he expected. He hadn't felt the anger building up in him before, but now it was overwhelming, crushing him like a tidal wave. "First, I had to come to this stupid island in the middle of nowhere, and now, finally, when I feel like I have a life here, I have to *leave*?"

"Alec, it's *dangerous*," she said, her voice finally cracking. "No one has any idea what's going on. I just want what's best—"

"Why do *you* get to decide what's best for me?" he said. "I just get carted around wherever's convenient."

"Sweetheart, you know that's not true," she said.

"You and Dad can ruin your own lives," he snapped. "Leave mine alone."

She closed her eyes, tears rolling down her face. The sight of her crying suddenly took all the heat out of his anger, making him feel sick and ashamed for yelling at her. He got up, ran out of the house, got on his bike, and rode into the gray hills of the island, into another blackout for all he cared.

He had his eyes closed and was finally beginning to make the writhing red cloud in his head calm down enough that he could hear the waves hitting Cathedral Rock, when Hannah called his name from behind him. He popped open his eyes and let the slopping gray ocean and churning clouds come back into view, with the off-white spires of the Rock connecting the two.

Hannah flopped down next to him. "Dude, have you heard of TikTok dances? I think that might be a thing I'm into—" She peered at his face. "Whoa. Alec, are you okay? Have you been crying?"

"I don't—" The rasp in his voice made him feel like a dweeb. He cleared his throat. "I don't think I'm

going to be able to help you guys stop the blackouts."
He told her the news, and how his mom had revealed
it. As he described it, Hannah put a hand on his arm,
and he almost broke down himself.

"That sucks, man," she said. "I'm so sorry. What
do you want to do?"

"What *can* I do?" he asked, shrugging. "Like, now
my dad's expecting me. My mom's all heartbroken and
miserable. What can I possibly say to either of them?"

"Say no," she said. "Tell them you're staying. What
is your mom going to do, force you onto that ferry?"

"I can't," he said. "She'll freak out, and cry,
and . . ." He sighed. "I don't want to make anyone
more miserable than they already are. I just feel like I
have no control."

"Alec, you're the *only* person here with any control," she said. "Dude, in the last two days, we've
fought a giant bug monster and found out the secret
of Derek's crazy great-grandfather. You're closer to
uncovering the secret of what's going on than *any*
grown-up here. You're not some . . ." She laughed and
gestured at the spires rising out of the water. "Some
rock that just gets molded by the elements. There, see,

you made me use a geology metaphor. If you don't want to get on that ferry, or live with your dad, you don't have to." When Alec didn't answer, she said, "*Do you want to go back?*"

"I dunno," he said. He hated that he wasn't sure, that he didn't have an answer. He was angry at his mother for trying to change his life without asking him . . . but the idea of going back, of seeing his old friends and old city and *Dad*, wasn't terrible. He did miss his life on the mainland, even if he was beginning to like the one he had here on Founders.

After a minute, Hannah sighed and said, "Well, look, the ferry you're supposed to leave on—that's tomorrow, after the morning blackout, right? Around four in the afternoon. You have until then to make up your mind."

"What do I do until then?" he asked.

Hannah gazed out at Cathedral Rock, and a smile crept across her face. "As long as you'll be here until the ferry leaves . . ."

15

DEPTHS

"This way," Derek half whispered, waving them down the dock. Alec and Hannah could only make out his silhouette through the fog, but the boy's broad shoulders and round head were recognizable even obscured by mist.

Alec had barely been able to sleep the night before, thinking about how he was going to deal with his mom's plans to send him back to the mainland. The minute the blackout was over—as light poured in through his window, he imagined Joan cracking her little eyes and smacking her chubby lips—he texted Hannah and told her to gather Derek and Checkmate so they could head out to Cathedral Rock ASAP. Derek agreed and told them where to meet him down on the harbor. Of course, Alec had shown up last, the only member of the party who hadn't compensated for the cloud of soup-thick fog that would be covering the island that early on a spring morning. It was like riding your bike through a charcoal drawing, he thought, everything turned to black, blurry shapes in the mist.

The Founders Island docks were old and water-eaten but had a sturdiness to them that seemed to have increased with the countless hurricanes they'd survived. Given that the island was all rocks and crab-grass, it didn't get any yachts or cruise ships rolling through, so the docks had been left to grow mossy and gray. The nicest boats anywhere were the white Rector Tours vessels off to one side, but even those looked dismal in the fog as Alec and Hannah walked past them.

Derek and Checkmate stood near a battered white boat, barely a dinghy, with a beat-up motor on the back and a coil of rope under the middle seat. Checkmate stared down at it skeptically, but Derek fussed with the knots tying it to the dock like the vessel had a pool table and minibar belowdecks. Alec saw that the boat even had a name printed on the side, and squinted to read it through the heavy fog and sloshing harbor water.

"The SS *Butt Kicker*," he said. "Classy, Derek."

"Oh, I'm sorry, do you own your own boat?" asked Derek sarcastically. "No? Tell you what, when you do, you can name it the *Bay Area Tech Dweeb* or whatever you like."

"And you're sure it'll get us out to Cathedral Rock and back in the fog?" asked Hannah.

"Most definitely," said Derek. "Me and this baby have been out there a lot. She'll serve our purposes. Did you bring the other stuff?"

Hannah shouldered off her backpack and tossed it in the boat. "Snorkels, goggles, and even a pair of flippers. If it's down there, I should be able to get it."

"Whoa, what?" asked Alec. He had assumed Hannah's text of *I'll bring the gear* meant some kind of long pole with a hook on the end. "You're *diving* down there to get the box? No way. That has to be dangerous."

"Hannah used to swim competitively," said Derek, rolling his eyes. "No one on the island's a better swimmer. She'll be fine."

"Really?" said Alec. "You don't have any trophies or anything in your room."

"Because there's nothing cooler than a gold statue with a barracuda on it," said Hannah. She stepped off the dock and into the swaying boat with the grace of a ballerina, then offered a hand to Alec. "Come on, time's a-wasting."

They piled into the boat one by one, Derek taking the rear. He ripped the cord on the motor, making the whole boat shudder to life, and then guided it slowly away from the dock and out into the foggy sea. Alec had to admit, he was impressed—Derek might have been a total goon, but he knew what he was doing on the water.

As the fog closed in around them, Alec thought back on everything they had experienced so far. They knew the green rocks were halves of the same thing, but that putting them together might have been what drove Derek's great-grandfather out of his mind. And according to Big Gran, putting the stones together also did something to the scrabblers, attracted them . . . which was weird, given how scared they were of the light on its own.

He thought again about the scrabblers' tattoos. That's what was still bothering him. He had to assume that giant bugs hadn't given each other tattoos, meaning those faces the creatures wore had belonged to actual humans once upon a time. So why'd they have the same tattoo?

The thought of a person transforming into a giant slime-shooting cave cricket made Alec wince with disgust. He wondered who the creatures were, before. Maybe if he and his friends solved the mystery of the blackout, the scrabblers wouldn't have to be bug monsters anymore, like ghosts with unfinished business. Another reason for them to figure this all out.

"Are you sure you know where we're going?" asked Hannah.

"Positive," said Derek, though he didn't sound very sure. Alec noticed he was gently moving the motor from side to side, steering them in a serpentine motion. "It should be out here . . ."

"Maybe we should wait until the fog lifts a little," said Alec.

"This time of year, the fog could hang around all afternoon," said Derek. "You wanna be out here when the next blackout hits? I don't think so—"

"Look out!" Hannah cried.

Cathedral Rock rose out of the haze all at once, going from dark patch to silhouette to hulking stone towers in a matter of seconds. Derek cursed, cut the motor, and veered hard to the right, missing a head-on collision but still slamming the side of his boat up against the rock where it met the water. They all held on to their seats as the dinghy swayed in the chop for a moment, but eventually it settled, and Alec could pry his aching grip off the boat and get a good look at the Rock itself.

This close, it was even taller than expected, with both of its towers reaching at least fifteen feet in the air. Its surface has a rough flakiness that was totally new to Alec, and it was full of large pores, some so big that he could've shoved his fist into the rock and never touched the sides. He heard a cry and looked up to see dozens of seabirds, mostly plump brown petrels, nesting in the upper pores of the towers; the area between the two towers was a huge smear of white and green with a pile of bird droppings. *That explains why people weren't allowed to walk on the rock when Derek's dad took them out here*, he thought.

Alec stared in awe. The structure, the shape, the fact that it was out in the ocean—everything about this rock was wrong, unlike any rock he'd ever read about. Between this and the green stone, there were unheard-of mineral formations present on Founders. They had to be connected . . . but how?

"Alec?" He snapped out of his haze and whirled around. Hannah was holding a mask and snorkel out to him. "Sorry, I know you're in geologist heaven right now, but the next blackout's in a few hours . . . if the schedule holds."

"Totally," he said, knowing that she was referring to Joan's sleep schedule. He pulled the mask over his eyes and popped the snorkel in his mouth. The others followed suit, their noses squished and lips bulging around their snorkels. Part of him wished he was getting in the water, actually going snorkeling, but Derek had been clear that he didn't want anyone but Hannah to get out of the boat. Besides, the water was supposed to be so cold at this time of year that it might give him hypothermia.

Hannah was the last and said in a nasal voice, "We all look down around the edge of the rock. If Derek's ancestor threw his stone out around here, he most likely did it right by the edge. Scan thoroughly, but be quick. We've got to go all around Cathedral until we find it. Remember, people used to throw a lot of stuff down there to make wishes, so keep your eyes peeled for something *unusual*."

Everyone nodded. They all got to the edge of the boat and knelt over the water.

"Three," counted Hannah, "two . . . one . . . go!"

Alec plunged his face into the sea.

Cold! He immediately understood why Derek didn't want anyone swimming today if they didn't have to. The ocean was icy, its sharp fingers digging right down to his scalp. Alec's breath hitched in his snorkel, and it took a moment for him to focus beyond the biting cold surrounding his head.

The bottom of the ocean around Cathedral Rock looked like an undersea graveyard. Huge stones surrounded the site, most fluttering with dark green seaweed and moss. Scattered between them were signs of humans—both the items that early settlers used to toss down by the rock to make wishes (lots of old coins, some rings, a locket or two, what appeared to be a lock of old hair in a brooch) and trash from careless tourists (soda cans, season-pass bracelets, a sun-bleached Transformers doll). The only animals around were small gray fish with big white eyes that darted between the stones like skittish ghosts.

After a little while, Hannah banged on the boat three times, and they all reared their heads back. Alec breathed in sharply as icy water rolled down his neck and into his shirt.

Hannah spat out her snorkel and said, "Anything?" They all shook their heads. "Me neither. All right, Derek, take us around."

Derek started up the motor again and eased them around the edge of the rock before the four of them stuck their heads back down into the brine. They kept going for what felt like hours, finding nothing with each patch of seafloor they looked down on.

Alec tried to focus on the task at hand, but his eyes kept getting dragged back to Cathedral Rock itself. There was something about the way it was connected to the ocean floor that bugged him—there was no curve up into the tower, none of the stripes or layers that would indicate erosion. That, plus the rocks all around it, basically made it look as though Cathedral Rock had fallen out of the sky and landed where it now sat.

They were about two-thirds of the way around the rock, and Alec was beginning to wonder if they'd ever get done before the next blackout, when Derek slapped the side of the boat and pointed into the water. Alec followed his finger . . . and saw it.

A metal box, some nine inches to a foot square, closed with an old-fashioned lock. It was overgrown with seaweed but visible if you were looking for it. And there was no way some lovesick well-wisher had lugged it all the way out there to throw it overboard.

They sat back and shed their goggles and snorkels. "Bet you ten to one there's the letters *RR* somewhere on that box," said Derek. "Think this is our best chance. You ready, Maplethorpe?"

"Gimme a sec," said Hannah. She shed her sweatshirt and pants, revealing a black wet suit. Then she yanked her goggles back on and put on the pair of flippers from her backpack. "Okay, I'm going to go down and get the box. If it's too heavy, I can come back up and get the rope, and we can all drag it up."

"Be careful," said both Alec and Derek at once. Alec glanced at him, and Derek looked away, red-faced.

Hannah smiled at Alec. "Bet you mainland kids don't do this very often."

"Oh, we all went diving for magical stones three years ago," said Alec. "You're way behind, Hannah."

"Keep an eye on me," she said, and then without hesitation sat on the rim of the boat and fell backward into the water.

Alec pulled his goggles on and shoved his head down in the cold. Hannah swam out over the box, floated for a moment—and then put out her hands and plummeted, kicking her way to the bottom. Alec was astounded to see his friend dive so deep like it was nothing; the box had to be at least twelve feet down.

Hannah grabbed the box and pulled up.

It didn't move.

She pulled again, and again, until finally she yanked as hard as she could, and he saw the seaweed covering it stretching—and then, finally, snapping. Hannah lifted up the box, smiling victoriously.

That was when he saw the rock move.

One of the big stones that had been sitting next to the box rolled slowly forward, landing with a muffled thud on top of Hannah's foot.

Alec watched his friend glance down at her flipper—and then look back up at him in sheer panic. She pulled, wiggled, dropped the box, and yanked at her leg, but the stone didn't budge.

Alec felt terror rocket through him as precious seconds passed and Hannah's foot still wasn't free.

She was stuck.

No one knew they were out there. If someone didn't help her, she'd run out of air.

Then, just like that, he was in the water.

Alec could barely believe it himself, but there he was, wheeling his arms, pulling himself deeper and deeper into the ocean. He'd never known cold like this, the ocean squeezing his body with a grip of ice. He rallied the heat in his limbs, spinning his arms and kicking his legs as hard as he could to reach Hannah.

When he finally got next to her, Hannah was frantically trying to shove the rock off her foot, and Alec could see her cheeks beginning to turn red with oxygen deprivation. Alec touched down on the other side of the rock and looped his arms around its cold, slimy surface. He pushed with his legs against the ocean floor, stretched his arms until they screamed with pain, felt every muscle in his body strain and a few of them pull or tear.

A grinding sensation, and the rock lifted. Hannah pulled her foot out from under it and pushed off hard against the bottom of the ocean, kicking up a cloud of silt as she shot toward the surface with the box clutched against her chest.

Alec did the same—and only rose about halfway. Frantically, he kicked and clawed at the water, making not nearly the same progress as his swimming-champ friend had. He began to feel the tightness of oxygen loss in his temples and behind his eyes, the cold of the water sinking deeper and deeper into his bones. Panic gripped him, and he shouted into his snorkel. He didn't want to die, not now, not here, trying to dig up buried treasure with Cathedral Rock looming over him like some giant, jagged animal's—

The Rock.

The realization hit Alec like a brick to the head.

He froze mid-stroke and peered at the porous surface of the rock, the angles and lines moving down it.

That was it . . .

A crash of water, and hands hooked under his shoulders.

The breath Alec sucked in upon breaking the surface was the most beautiful thing he'd ever tasted. He slid, coughing and sputtering, back onto the floor of the boat, spilling icy water everywhere as he went.

Once he'd caught his breath and the colored spots had cleared away from his vision, he looked back to find out who'd pulled him out—and was surprised to see Derek, soaked and panting, sprawled behind him.

"Thanks," he coughed.

"Whatever," said Derek, standing and wringing out his shirt. "Can't have someone die on one of our family's boats. My dad would murder me." He took up his spot at the motor, yanked the thing to life, and steered them back toward the island.

Alec finally got a chance to look at the box in Hannah's arms. The thing was dented and battered, and thick, slimy hunks of seaweed still dangled from its face. But it remained unrusted, and its lid bore the initials *R R* above the latch.

"Looks like we're on the right track," said Alec through chattering teeth.

"You stopped," said Hannah. "Why?"

"What?" he asked.

"On your way up, you stopped swimming," she said. "You saw something. What was it?"

"Nothing," he said, shaking his head and looking away from her. He couldn't say it out loud, not yet. It was totally ridiculous. He had to be sure, anyway, to have his suspicions confirmed before he mentioned it.

After all, how would Hannah react?

Would she believe him when he told her that Cathedral Rock was a giant tooth, sitting out in the middle of the ocean?

16

THE PULSE

They could see the docks up ahead when Hannah checked her phone and swore.

"What's up?" asked Alec.

"Nothing," she sighed. "My mom's texting me, saying Big Gran's upset. She's probably angry I borrowed the stone again. I'll just let her know I'll have it back around . . ." She froze, her mouth hanging open. Her eyes fluttered between her phone and Alec.

"What's up?" said Alec, hugging himself a little

tighter. He wished he'd worn a wet suit like Hannah; with the sea breeze whipping at him, he felt almost as cold as he had in the ocean. His toes were nearly numb—next time, he told himself, he'd take off his shoes before diving in the water—and his teeth couldn't stop chattering.

"It's eleven thirty-two," said Hannah.

Somehow, those words made Alec feel colder than he could've possibly imagined.

"It's naptime," he said softly.

"We need to get onshore, now," said Hannah. She looked over Alec's shoulder at Derek. "How long until we get on dry land?"

Derek shrugged and gestured toward the shore. "The docks are right there. Calm down."

"This took longer than we thought," she said. "It's almost noon. The next blackout will hit any minute now."

Derek's eyes widened. He leaned on the motor, making its mechanical hum go high-pitched and frantic, like the buzz of a giant wasp that just got angry.

They docked hurriedly and silently, as though mentioning the blackout out loud would somehow cause it to happen. They power-walked up the dock, which was thankfully abandoned, the four of them being the only ones willing to risk walking down by the water so close to the next appointed blackout time.

They could see the parking lot in the distance, and Alec could pick his bike out of those lined up at the metal rack—when Alec felt his teeth buzz, and the whole world plunged into darkness.

The four of them stopped dead in their tracks. The parking lot that Alec had just seen a short walk away now might as well be in New Zealand.

"Wait for it," said Hannah.

Hannah's backpack began to glow, faintly at first and then brightly. At the same time, green light began to spill out from under the lid of the metal box clutched to her chest.

"Well, at least we know it's in there," said Derek.

"If only we could get that lock open," said Alec.

"Are you kidding?" Derek laughed. "That thing's, what, ninety years old? Checkmate, you're up."

In the faint green glow, Checkmate took the box from Hannah and put it under his arm like a football. He grabbed the lock in his free hand, pulled it—and

SNAP, the metal ring broke, and the old, worn lock fell to pieces. He gingerly held up the box and opened the lid—and light blasted outward in a sturdy beam.

It was the other half of their rock, Alec instantly knew—it bore the same smooth, slightly tarnished surface, with one end jagged and shiny. But if anything, the stone seemed to glow even brighter than Big Gran's did, sending a radiant green light out of the box that lit up much of the docks around them. He wondered if it was actually brighter on its own, or if maybe being near its other half was increasing the energy output.

A few yards away, there was a lonesome howl. Their heads turned toward it . . . and then back to the rock.

"Let's see if this baby works as well as its twin brother," said Derek. He snatched up the rock and, before any of them could argue or protest, jogged off toward the noise.

They came upon the scrabbler before it knew what was happening. The creature shrieked and cowered as Derek shoved the stone in front of it. This one wore a man's face, with tousled blond locks hanging clumped around the rotten eye sockets and dangling lower jaw—and, Alec noted, the small mark beneath one eye that might be a tattoo if he got close enough to see. The creature flicked its abdomen toward Derek and tried to hit him with thick gobs of its gooey secretion, but Derek was ready for it now and dodged the giant boogers easily before thrusting the light in its eyes again.

Derek kept advancing, until soon the creature was a balled mass of legs, hissing and whimpering as it hid its face beneath its hands. For the first time since he'd discovered the horrible monsters, Alec felt sorry for one.

"That's enough, Derek," he said, his voice sounding small in the huge darkness around them. "Look at it, it's terrified."

"Aw, shut up, newbie." Derek laughed. "Let's try to squash this bug! Maplethorpe, give me the other half of the stone. Let's see if it'll hurt this thing."

"Alec's right, Derek," said Hannah. When Derek didn't move, she stormed over and grabbed at his hand, yelling, "Derek, leave it *alone*—"

It was so quick, Alec didn't see it until it was over: Derek grabbed Hannah's backpack, and with one strong shove, threw her out of it so that she stumbled to the ground while he held on to the bag. It was a bully's move, he thought, practiced over years and years of shoving kids like Alec out of their backpacks so they could be inspected for lunch money and desserts.

"Hey!" shouted Hannah, but already Derek had ripped open the bag and pulled out the other green stone. He held the two broken sides up, matching them right. For a second, Alec could swear he saw crackles of lightning between the two pieces, drawing them to each other.

Derek shoved the two halves together, re-forming a single, kidney-bean-shaped rock.

The glow began to pulse.

Instead of a strong, solid glow, it flickered like a heartbeat. With it, there was a noise that Alec couldn't hear so much as feel deep in his ears and in his teeth, a heavy vibration that grew stronger with every throb of the light.

The scrabbler stopped shivering instantly. Slowly, it rose from its cowering crouch, stood on its many legs, and turned to them. When Alec saw its face, he groaned and reared back, horrified.

The scrabbler's eyes had turned totally white. And they were fixed on the pulsing light of the stone.

With careful steps, the creature crept toward them. From its open mouth came a low moan, like the howl they'd heard before but ten octaves lower. "Stay back!" cried Derek, shoving the rock toward it, but the scrabbler wasn't scared. Now it seemed *interested*, slowly reaching its hands out toward the glow. When Derek yanked it away from the scrabbler, the thing's head turned to follow it, those zombie eyes never leaving the pulsing light.

"Guys!" called Hannah. Alec whipped around and saw his friend pointing off into the dark around them. Alec heard more low moaning, a chorus slowly building in the night.

Eyes appeared in the dark. White and luminous, glittering in the pulsing green light.

Coming toward them.

One by one, dead, openmouthed faces emerged from the shadows, and behind them a forest of arched, feathery legs. Each face was different—a chubby old mustached head here, a freckled young girl there, the woman that had snotted up Alec's hand—but they were all bloated and lifeless, and every single one of them bore a key tattoo under their left eye. Wherever

Alec and his friends turned, a new scrabbler was emerging from the dark, moving at the same deliberate crawl, all with the same clam-white eyes and low, hungry moans.

Alec couldn't believe how many of them there were—two dozen, maybe more. He kept backing away from the ones nearest him, until his shoulder collided with Checkmate's arm. Then he felt Hannah's and Derek's backs against theirs, and it hit him.

They were surrounded.

There was nowhere to go.

"Guys, what do we do?" asked Hannah.

"Pull the rocks apart," said Alec. "Use the light." But a glance showed Derek frantically clawing at the seam between the two halves. It told Alec everything he needed to know. Whatever the rocks were, they were a single unit now.

The ring of scrabblers grew so tight that Alec couldn't even make out their insect bodies anymore, just a ring of severed heads with blank eyes and gaping mouths. This close, Alec could see the boils on one scrabbler's eyebrow, the gold tooth shining out of another's swinging lower jaw. He closed his eyes tight, and hoped whatever was about to happen would be quick.

"Back."

The moaning stopped.

Alec's eyes snapped open. Around him, the scrabblers were frozen in place.

Was that voice real? Had he imagined it?

"*Back*, I say."

One by one, the huge creatures crept away, their heads bowed and thin arms folded mantis-like at their chests. As the horde parted, Alec saw a new shape in the pulsing green glow—the shape of a man, approaching them.

He was tall and stately, his square chin held high and his chest puffed out. A black coat with long tails and two columns of silver buttons hung from his broad shoulders, though its ragged collar and threadbare elbows showed that it had seen better days. That, plus the kerchief at his neck and his dark hair tied into a ponytail, made Alec think he was dressed up in a historical costume, like a man reenacting the Civil War. But what took him aback was the figure's eyes, huge and hazel, focused on them with an intense sort of purpose.

As the man reached them, he turned and held out a hand to the scrabblers. The creatures retreated even further, though their eyes still glittered at the edge of the darkness.

"Poor wretches," rumbled the man in a deep voice. "They cannot stay away from the bezoar. They know it's the only thing that can save them."

"Dude, who the heck are *you*?" asked Derek.

The man turned back to them, and a tight smile crossed his lips.

"Forgive my manners," he said, and extended a large, calloused hand. "I am Rochester Erickson. This is my island."

17

FOUNDERS

The four kids stared silently at the figure. After a moment, he retracted his hand and sighed.

"I understand your disbelief," he said.

"Rochester Erickson is *dead*, dude," said Hannah. "He's been dead since the 1800s."

The man nodded, a knowing look crossing his face. "Missing, actually. Though with time being what it is in this realm of endless night, I suppose missing and dead are really the same." He glanced around him, then back at the kids. "And if you are in this impenetrable gloom with me . . . then it would be 2021 now, would it not?"

"That's right," said Alec. Slowly, he stepped away from the huddle of his friends and stood before the man. Something clicked in his head as he thought about the man in front of him. "It coincides with your comet, doesn't it?"

He nodded. "Precisely. A masterful deduction, Mr. . . ."

"Xiang," said Alec. "Alec Xiang."

"A pleasure, Master Xiang," said Erickson. "I am pleased that young men as intelligent as you live on the island I discovered—"

"Sorry, hold up," said Hannah, stepping forward. "How do we know you're really Rochester Erickson? I mean, if you were, or *are*, what would you be doing *here*? In the blackout?"

Erickson smiled broadly. "Only a Maplethorpe would be so direct. Young lady, you are the spitting image of your ancestors. The answer to why I am here is, I'm afraid, somewhat complicated." He gestured off into the shadows. "Shall we walk?"

"It's dark out there," said Derek. "And there are probably more of those things waiting for us."

"Young Master Rector, I have walked this island in the dark for many a silent hour," he said. "I know my way around. And as for these poor mutations, do not worry. They know me and would not harm those in my company."

"They *know* you?" asked Derek.

A sorrowful expression crossed the man's face. "I'm afraid," he said, "they made up most of the original party that I brought with me to this island." And with that, he turned and walked off into the dark, leaving the kids to follow him.

"What do you think?" Alec whispered to Hannah as they walked close behind Erickson, the man's coattails always threatening to slip off into the dark and vanish entirely.

"Are you asking if I trust Sleepy Hollow up there? No," she said, but then sighed. "But he did know my name, and Derek's. And as long as he keeps those monsters at bay, we might as well roll with him."

Alec nodded and hugged himself . . . but he wasn't that cold, he realized, even if he was damp.

He hadn't thought about it before, but the blackouts were never as cold as they should be, so devoid of light and electricity. They were warm, even. The idea made him uneasy, and he picked up the pace.

"So, sorry to be kinda direct, but what exactly is going on here?" Derek asked Erickson.

"Are you familiar with the hermetic arts, Master Rector?" asked Erickson, marching straight ahead.

"Um . . . not as much as I'd like to be?" said Derek.

"Perhaps that's for the best," Erickson replied. "When we came here, my fellow settlers and I were practicing forms of Eastern medicine and elemental alchemy that we thought would turn this rock into paradise."

"Sounds a lot like witchcraft," said Alec.

"To some, perhaps," said Erickson, waving his hand dismissively. "But any magic with a positive end should be at least understood. Founders Island was to be a utopia. A place where mankind's hunger and greed would be vanquished, and the ways of old would flourish. We believed the coming of the comet would open a doorway to a perfect world . . . and in a way, it did." He sighed. "Unfortunately, it also slammed the door shut behind us."

"So you got trapped here? In the blackout?" asked Hannah. "Some perfect world."

"You're correct in mocking us, Miss Maplethorpe," said Erickson. "But there are layers of this dark, depths you cannot see. For whatever reason, I was caught in one where I remained human, if alone in some strange dimension. But it had a profound effect on my cohorts. As you see, they quickly began to transform into the strange creatures that have been roaming your countryside." He shook his head. "Even Samuel Gareen, my dearest friend, was lost to this darkness. He was a brave man, who shared my vision more than anyone. And he, too, became one of the lost."

"You mean the *scrabblers*," said Hannah.

Erickson stopped in his tracks, and a sad smile crossed his face. "I have not heard that term for them since your young ancestor Henrietta appeared before me. Is she still with us?"

"A hundred and five years old," said Hannah.

"Extraordinary." Erickson shook his head again. "If only she and the Rector boy had been able to help us. But they were young, mere babes. Not like you."

They continued walking in silence a while longer, trudging uphill in the warm, pulsing green light, until Alec couldn't take it any longer. "Where are we going?"

"Just up here, Master Xiang," said Erickson, pointing. "This hilltop. It will provide us with the perfect view."

The ground finally leveled out, and Alec felt a breeze cross his face. They *were* on a hilltop, he realized, one of the hills over by Sawtooth Cliffs. He and Hannah had come here before, eaten chips and watched the ferry bob in and out of the harbor. It was definitely a spot for an excellent view . . . and, he thought, further proof that the figure walking with them knew the island well enough to be its founder.

"Master Rector, hold the bezoar high over your head here," Erickson instructed.

"The what?" said Derek.

"The bezoar—the stone," said the man with a small, pitying smile. "Raise it high. In fact, perhaps your silent friend should be the one to do so. He has rather long limbs."

Checkmate had been so quiet that Alec had forgotten he was there. Derek held the pulsing rock out to him, and slowly—reluctantly, thought Alec—he stepped forward and took it.

Checkmate raised the stone over his head, and the pulse of the light seemed to quicken, with each wave of light glowing brighter than the last. Erickson looked toward the sky . . . and then pointed with one hand.

"There," he said. "The comet beckons."

Alec's eyes rose up to the sky, and he couldn't help but gasp. Overhead, in the starless blackness, the comet blazed like a radioactive smear across the heavens. It was longer than he'd expected it to be, every inch of its tail twinkling behind it in a flaming line. Maybe on a normal night, only parts of it could be seen, but in the lightless sky, every particle burned bright.

The stone began pulsing so hard it was officially flashing. The comet's light flickered brighter and brighter.

"Now watch!" called Erickson. "It will show us. It will use its energy to reveal—"

There was a blinding flash as a bolt of green lightning flared across the sky, seeming to come out of the comet itself. It lit up the whole island for an instant, but its trajectory was certain. In that split second of brightness, all the other buildings on the island were just shadowy silhouettes . . .

But the Honeycomb was clearly visible.

Oh no, thought Alec.

"There," said Erickson eagerly, pointing out into the dark toward Hannah's house. "There, in that home. That way lies the sleeper. We must go to them."

"The sleeper?" asked Derek.

"A babe," said Erickson, turning toward them. "No more than a year old. There's one in every generation, and when they sleep, their dreams bring this world and yours together. They are the key to this island's salvation. To my own ascension."

"But that's . . ." Derek paused, and an angry scowl crossed his brow. He looked back at Hannah, open-mouthed, unbelieving.

"Quickly, my friends," said Erickson. "We must go there. We must find the child. Before—"

"We—we can't," said Hannah.

Erickson glared at her. "Really. Why not?"

Alec took a step toward Hannah. He saw it now,

finally—the weird vibe he'd gotten from Erickson so far, that little something that he couldn't quite put his finger on. Now he could see it clear as day in Erickson's eyes as the pulsing light reflected in them.

The guy wanted something. He had plans of his own.

"The blackouts only last for about an hour in the afternoon," said Hannah. She gulped. "This one will be over soon. Our families don't know we're out here. If they get worried, they'll come looking for us. And that will interfere with whatever comes next."

Erickson stared coldly at her for a moment longer . . . and then nodded and rubbed his hands together vigorously.

"Quite right," he said. "Quite right. Very well, my young friends. Tonight, when the darkness has arrived once more, bring the sleeper to me. We must go to the wood along Hobble Ridge to finish the ritual. Then we can finally banish this curse and fulfill our destinies."

"We'll try to make it," said Alec. "It's just . . . we're kids, you know? We have to sneak out and stuff."

Erickson fixed those cold eyes on Alec. Again, Alec could see the hunger behind the man's kindness and flowery speech, the complete focus on getting what he desired.

"I pray you don't make me wait," he said.

All at once, light swept across the island. The four friends stood on the hill alone, Founders sprawled on all sides of them.

It was then that Alec noticed that Derek hadn't stopped glowering at them.

"Sorry, but real quick," he said, quiet and furious. "Is Hannah's little sister causing the blackouts?"

18

THE KEY

The silence after Derek's question was somehow deeper and more complete than the quiet of the blackout they'd just left. Hannah and Alec froze, trying to think of answers, with only distant waves and whistling wind to soundtrack them.

"It's more complicated than that," said Hannah.

"Are you *kidding me*?" exploded Derek. He launched across the hill, his cheeks red and eyes bright. "Hannah, all of our neighbors are losing their minds, everyone's job is in danger, and you've *known what's been causing the blackouts all along*? And you didn't *tell us*?!"

"Watch it, Derek—" Alec stepped between Derek and Hannah, and Derek shoved him aside like he was nothing.

"She's my little sister, Derek," said Hannah. "If everyone knew she was related to the blackouts, she wouldn't be safe."

"Look around you!" he shouted. "*None of us* are safe! People are going to lose their houses, and their jobs." Derek's mouth turned down hard at the edges, and Alec could see tears shining in the corners of his eyes. "*My* folks, Hannah. My folks are going to lose their business, they can't pay the mortgage, they fight every day . . . my dad *cries*." He sniffed, wiped at his eyes, and looked all the more furious. "And you didn't help us. You thought of yourself and your family before anyone else."

"Derek, I'm sorry, but she's a *baby*," said Hannah. Her face looked surprised and hurt to Alec, shocked by Derek's breakdown. "Keeping her up all night's not a possibility. If people in town find out, they might even try to take her away from us. What can I do?"

"Let's take her out tonight, then," said Derek. He nodded behind him, to where Erickson had last stood. "Have Rochester do whatever magic he's gotta do to break this spell. Then it'll be done for."

A conflicted expression flashed across Hannah's face, but Alec instantly knew the answer in his gut. "We can't do that," he said.

"No one asked you!" snapped Derek, turning and wheeling on him with a fist raised. Alec winced but managed to stand his ground.

"There's something wrong with that guy, Derek," Alec pressed. "He didn't give us any real answers to our questions, or explain any of this. The comet, the blackouts . . . we still know as much as we did before. He just told us how we could help him. And now he wants us to bring a baby to the *woods*? Something doesn't add up here."

Derek's mouth worked in tight circles, like he was trying to hock up a good response and spit it on Alec, but he finally cursed and turned away.

"Tell you what," he said, storming back toward the docks. "If you want your green rock back, you'll meet us outside your place tonight at eight. Have your little sister with you. Come on, Checkmate. Bring that stone."

Checkmate looked at the stone in his hand, then back at Derek . . . and shook his head.

"Checkmate, we're leaving!" snapped Derek, his cheeks glowing with rage.

Again, the tall boy shook his head, his face remaining as calm and still as ever. When Derek took a step back toward him, he tossed the stone to Hannah. She narrowly caught it and quickly stuffed it in her backpack.

Derek threw up his hands and chuckled meanly. "Great. Last time I make friends with some silent treatment *freak*. If you'll excuse me, I gotta go find another way to keep my family from becoming homeless."

Derek stormed off, shouldering Alec hard as he went. They watched him go, a bitter look crossing Hannah's face as he climbed onto his bike and rode off.

"What a jerk," said Alec.

Hannah shook her head. "No . . . well, maybe. But he's just scared." She sniffed and knuckled her eye. "I wish I could help him. Everyone, the whole island. I just don't know how that wouldn't put Joan in jeopardy."

"We'll figure it out," said Alec, not sure he believed himself. "First things first, we've got to find a way to stop this without letting your sister get hurt. Or at the very least, we've got to figure out what Erickson wants to do with her."

Hannah nodded, hard and fast. "Right, right. But how? Where can we find information about our island's ghost founder and ancient magic rituals?"

Checkmate whistled between his teeth and waved them on as he walked toward his bike. Hannah and Alec shared a look, unsure if they should follow the huge kid—and then they slowly began walking with him.

"I didn't even know we had a library," said Alec as they pulled into the small parking lot.

"It's not a very popular hangout," said Hannah. Alec understood why: The Founders Island Public Library was a square two-story building, set a few streets away from everything on Marina Boulevard. It was built into the side of a hill, so that the building seemed to look down on them even while it was tiny, like a little kid trying to play bully. Most of it was solid gray stone, though one wing had floor-to-ceiling windows on sharp diagonals that looked as though they were trying to be modern. But the glass was now so cloudy that Alec couldn't see inside, and the chrome edges were eaten away with rust.

Alec knew the inside would be nothing like the San Francisco Public Library, where he'd gone with his school—floor after floor of sweeping books in beautiful, modern architecture—but he wasn't ready for just how depressing the place was. This library had cream-colored walls, faded shag carpet, the overpowering sour smell of old books, and even a children's nook with a ripped beanbag chair and a mural of poorly copied characters from *Rugrats* and *Pokémon* along the wall.

"Why are we here?" he grumbled at Hannah.

"I don't know," she said. "I haven't been here since second grade. We should ask—"

"Eli?" Behind the front desk stood a pale woman with a round, kind face and bright, inquisitive eyes. She glanced nervously from Checkmate to Alec and Hannah, then back again. "Is everything all right, sweetheart? I thought you were going to be home for the blackout." Checkmate shook his head and motioned off into the library. His mom nodded, then smiled at Alec and Hannah. "Let me know if you need help finding anything."

"Actually, Ms. Berger," said Hannah, "do you have any books on the history of Founders Island?"

Ms. Berger's face brightened. "We have many, actually—" Then it fell. "But they're all in use. You'll find them with Mr. Blackwing in the back."

Checkmate led them through the library like he lived there, weaving his huge frame easily between shelves and tables. Finally, he waved them down a narrow aisle between two shelves, and they popped out near a small reading desk in the corner of the modern addition, light pouring dimly through the windows. The desk was piled with thick books and packets of paper between them, making up sandwiches of pure boring.

Hunched in the midst of it all was Andre Blackwing, the historian from the town meeting. He typed intently on a laptop, pausing every so often to check a small stack of printouts at his elbow and thumb his long black hair behind his ear.

"Um, Mr. Blackwing?" asked Hannah.

"Gyah!" Blackwing sat up with a start, sending his printouts fluttering to the floor. He whirled, brushed his hair out of his face, and after a moment broke into a sly smile. "Geez, kids, you scared me. I mean, I know Boo Radley over there is good at sneaking up on people, but I didn't realize he was teaching his classmates to do it, too."

"Sorry to bother you," Hannah said. "We just were wondering if we could ask you a few questions about the history of Founders Island. And Rochester Erickson."

Blackwing gestured to the towers of books around him. "You might have to be a bit more specific, kid. Everything I'm working on right now is about this island's history. And as for Erickson, well, I'm sure you learned a lot about him in school."

"Yeah, and a great man he was," said Alec. "But what we're wondering—"

"Well, no," said Blackwing. "But go on."

"Sorry, what?" asked Alec.

"Erickson," said Blackwing. "Not a very good guy. In fact, today we'd consider him a total psychopath.

But hey, founded the island we're all on, so you take the good with the bad."

Alec felt a sharp prickle along his neck and arms. He'd known it, staring into that man's eyes—that there was something wrong, something they weren't being told. "Erickson wasn't a good man?"

Blackwing laughed and turned back to his desk. He scanned the spines of the books that made up his fortress of research, then pulled out a thick one with a green canvas cover. Alec got a glance of the title, embossed in gold—*Cult Worship in the Americas*.

"You ever heard of the Order of the Obsidian Gate?" asked Blackwing, flipping through the book.

"Afraid not," said Hannah.

"Yeah, I'm not surprised," said Blackwing. "So, basically, the Order was a doomsday cult that believed in performing these weird rituals to try and raise an ancient god they called Ichthyon. Real nasty sucker, who was supposed to have come here from space, lived before modern history, wanted to spread darkness all over the world, all that jazz." He stopped flipping and then held the book out to them. "Take a look—this was their symbol."

Alec stared at the page and felt his mouth go dry.

Over the chapter heading was a black drawing of a key.

The same key he'd seen on the faces of the scrabblers.

"Why a key?" Alec asked, his eyes unable to leave the drawing.

"Ah, that was their whole thing," said Blackwing. "They were gonna discover the key to open the gate to bring Ichthyon back into the world. Which basically meant let this monster god back on Earth so it could get its revenge on all the sniveling primates who live here now. Part of the reason Erickson came here was because he thought this island was full of magical items—special herbs, bezoars, that kind of stuff."

"Bezoars!" cried Hannah, and the whole crew hunched their shoulders at the sound of a long "Sssssshhhhhh" from Checkmate's mom off in the stacks. "What are those?"

This one Alec knew. "Special stones," he said. "People thought touching them could cure all sorts of diseases. Sometimes formed in the earth but usually found in the stomachs of large animals."

"Awful," said Hannah. "Another point on the board for geology, nerd. Okay, so, Erickson was a member of this cult?"

"His dad *started* the whole thing," said Blackwing, grinning like a kid telling an especially dark ghost story. "Kristoff Gareen was the guy's name. Said he uncovered some ancient tablets saying this creature was the rightful ruler of the world. Got super into it, convinced a bunch of people to give him all their money and possessions, and somewhere along the way he had little Sammy."

"Sammy?" asked Alec.

"Rochester's real name," said Blackwing. "Sam Gareen, heir to the monster cult. Spent about half his teens in an asylum, he was so obsessed with the idea of bringing about the end of the world."

Erickson's words rocketed back into Alec's mind. *Even Samuel Gareen, my dearest friend, was lost to this darkness. He was a brave man, who shared my vision more than anyone.*

"He was a con man," said Alec, the words feeling chalky as he spoke them.

"Yeah, but before he took on the name Rochester

and started playing founding father, he really believed it," said Blackwing. "Of course, none of this is proven—it's all a rumor I'm chasing. I think that's why he came out here. He thought the island was somehow part of the key." He turned the page in the book, grabbed a printout from his desk, and held the two next to each other. "There's kind of a resemblance, don't you think?"

On the right was a portrait of Rochester Erickson, one Alec had seen dozens of times since he'd gotten here, with his head held high and the sea behind him. It shook him to see how much it looked like the ghostly man they'd just spoken to in the blackout.

The other was a portrait of Samuel Gareen, almost certainly the same man, in a black coat, wide-brimmed hat, and bushy mustache. But what was most different was the atmosphere around this second portrait, a vague sense that the artist knew something was wrong with this guy. The background was dark, stormy gray, and in his eyes shown a brightness that told Alec to keep a distance from whoever he was.

"Oh no," said Hannah with a gasp. She pointed at the portrait of Gareen. "Alec, look at his hand."

His eyes followed the second portrait's outstretched hand.

It rested on a human skull. Clutched in the fingers was an iron key.

"It's the First Man," Alec said, feeling something quiver deep in his guts. "From Robert Rector's journal. The one he said we shouldn't trust. He's behind all of this."

"Robert Rector?" asked Blackwing. "Like, who used to live here? You have his *journal*? That could be really important to my work—"

"We need to find Derek," said Hannah. "We need to let him know. Maybe then we can come up with a plan. Come on."

"Wait, wait, guys," said Blackwing, holding a hand up to them. A strange expression of knowing had crossed his face, as though he was beginning to put pieces together. "What do you know about Erickson that I don't?"

Alec chewed on the idea. They couldn't get adults involved . . . but he didn't want to leave the guy hanging.

"There's a third verse to the 'Founders Hymn' that no one knows about carved in the basement of the school," Alec said as they headed for the door.

"That ought to buy us some time," mumbled Hannah as they left.

19

Lovely, Dark, and Deep

Derek Rector was a ghost.

They tried every store downtown, every inch of the hills around his house, even down by the water again, where people were already beginning to line up for the last ferry to the mainland. Alec recognized many of their faces from around town, but today all were scowling and sighing and staring balefully down at their luggage. They were fleeing, he knew, leaving their homes until things got under control, and they weren't happy about it. Greg Walia sat on a bench next to his parents, his shiner looking significantly less nasty. Hannah asked him if he'd seen Derek, but the kid just shook his head.

"This isn't good," said Hannah as Alec and Checkmate pulled their bikes up next to her on their way to Sawtooth Cliffs. "You shouldn't be able to hide on an island like this. If we can't find him, it means he's avoiding us."

Alec nodded, but his mind was elsewhere. Going down to the docks had reminded him that *he* was supposed to be on that ferry, that he should have been home packing over an hour ago. Part of him wondered if he should just break off and call it, apologize to Hannah, head home and hug his mom goodbye, and get ready to see his dad again . . .

But he couldn't. Something about that felt wrong, like taking the easy route when the hard one was more important. Maybe it was because for the first time in forever, he was doing what *he* wanted to do. His mom was probably trying to find him, just like they were trying to find Derek. But his phone was off and he didn't dare turn it back on. No one was steering his bike but him, and the only people by his side were his friends, old and new.

He sighed. That would all feel very heroic . . . if he wasn't so scared about what was going to happen the next time Hannah's little sister fell asleep.

Derek wasn't at the cliffs, either; the only people there were two old men listening to the waves. As he and Hannah remounted their bikes, Alec felt his stomach growl, and it dawned on him that he hadn't eaten since his extra-early breakfast.

"Any chance we can swing by the Honeycomb and grab a bite?" he asked. Checkmate gave him an emphatic thumbs-up.

"Sure, let's just be quick," said Hannah. "We have to get to Derek before the blackout hits. But I bet we have some leftover stew around."

As they biked up the long, winding road to the Honeycomb, Hannah's mother came out of the house, frustration across her face. She shouted at them as they came up to the front steps, though Alec couldn't catch what she was saying over the wind in his ears— probably griping at them for being out during the blackout, or announcing that Alec's mom had called.

"Sorry, what's up, Mom?" asked Hannah as they pulled up front.

"I said, where is she?" asked Hannah's mom. "I don't know why you're back here, after all the fuss. First we had to wait until Big Gran dozed off, then we had to get her riding seat onto his bike—and now you're back here? I don't have *time* for this, Hannah."

"Mom, what are you talking about?" asked Hannah.

Her mom blinked, some of the anger on her face turning into confusion. "Derek Rector told me about your picnic with baby Joan."

Alec felt his heart skip a beat. Checkmate slapped a hand to his forehead.

"How long ago did he take her?" asked Hannah.

A flash of panic crossed her mom's face. "About twenty minutes ago. He said you were having a picnic in the woods under Hobble Ridge—"

They were back on their bikes in seconds, speeding down the road with Hannah in the lead. Alec's breath ripped hot and angry through his lungs, but he didn't dare slow down, just kept pushing himself and picturing chubby-cheeked Joan on her way to God knows where.

"We've got to find them before he's on his bike for too long," shouted Hannah.

"Why?" asked Alec.

"Because riding in her bike seat puts Joan to sleep," snapped Hannah.

Alec found the strength and pedaled even faster.

They came over a hill, and Hobble Ridge loomed up ahead, complete with the brooding pine woods huddling between it and St. Brendan's. Even with everything going on, the sight of the Ridge gave Alec a shudder. Before, it had just been a bizarre phenomenon; now, after everything he'd learned, something about the way it rose up out of the island and curved over the woods struck him as sinister. It was like the Ridge disapproved of the church below it and towered over it threateningly. He thought about Cathedral Rock, how it looked just like a giant tooth, and wondered what secret force had created this bizarre and menacing—

"There!" shouted Hannah, swerving at she pointed frantically.

A ways down the road, Derek pedaled hard on his bike.

On the back was strapped a bike seat, and in it a tiny bundle.

They rode hard, using the gravity of the rolling hills to propel them forward. "Derek, stop!" called Hannah, but the sound of her voice only made him pedal more furiously, and before they knew it, he had rounded the back of St. Brendan's and was out of sight.

They skidded around the church and scraped to a halt in the lot out back. Derek's bike lay abandoned on its side, but Alec could hear him in the distance, crunching his way through the ferns and sticks of the forest. For a moment, he thought about how much he'd wanted to go for a long nature walk in these woods once summer rolled around—and then he was running into the shade of the trees, Hannah and Checkmate flanking him.

Instantly, they were bathed in gloom, the thick trunks and heavy pine boughs throwing cool shadows over them. Once again, Alec felt something was wrong; he couldn't help but think that the trees almost felt too big, their branches too thick, the ferns around them taller and tougher than they should be. It was like the whole forest was on steroids, a prehistoric wood that time forgot.

He came around the edge of a trunk—and froze.

Derek sat on a felled tree a few yards ahead, his back to them. His shoulders bounced lightly, but he made no indication that he knew he'd been spotted.

Alec waved Hannah and Checkmate over, holding a finger up to his lips. When they saw Derek, they nodded and motioned for Alec to make the first move.

Alec tiptoed forward—and instantly stepped on a fern. The whole forest echoed with the crunch.

Derek looked up over his shoulder, but there was no panic or worry in his eyes. He kept bouncing, though—and as he turned to face them, Alec saw why.

Joan lay in his arms, a pacifier bobbing in her mouth, a pair of headphones over her head that connected to an iPhone lying on her chest. She blinked slowly once . . . twice . . .

"No!" yelled Alec, leaping for Derek—

Then Joan's eyes closed, and all was darkness.

Alec ate it, tripping over his own feet and crashing into a pile of ferns and dead pine boughs. As he tried to sit up and spit some of the needles off his face, he saw the stone's green light pulse in the forest, making the trees look extra tall and the shadows between them endlessly dark. As Hannah helped him up, Checkmate held out the stone, illuminating Derek. The boy was now standing and facing them, Joan clutched to his chest.

"Derek, this is out of control," Alec said once he was back on his feet. "Just give us the baby. We can figure this out."

"Shut up, newbie," said Derek calmly, his face still with blank contempt. "You're not from here. What you think doesn't matter."

"Joan!" screamed Hannah at the top of her lungs. *"Joan! Wake up, Joan!"*

Derek shook his head. "Your mom says this is her favorite binky, and I've got a playlist of relaxing classical music over four hours long. Unless you have an air horn, she's not waking up anytime soon."

"Please, Derek," Hannah sobbed. "Please don't hurt her, she's my sister, she's just a *baby*—"

"I'm not going to hurt her," said Derek, looking offended. "How can you even say that, Hannah? I would *never* hurt Joan. Your mom and dad, you, everyone on this island—they're like my family. I don't want to hurt anyone." He inhaled sharply, his nostrils flaring. "And that's why we just need to listen to what Erickson says and stop the blackouts."

"Derek, Erickson isn't trying to stop the blackouts," said Alec. "Actually, he's probably trying to keep them going. He's not a good dude."

Derek blinked, his stern expression breaking for a moment. "What do you mean? Rochester Erickson started the town. He's the *founder* of Founders Island."

"Actually, he's some sort of weird monster worshipper," said Alec. "And Rochester Erickson isn't even his real name. It's—"

"That's enough."

Alec's words left his throat with a gasp. He and the others whirled as a chorus of throaty clicks closed in around them.

The scrabblers had them surrounded, creeping through the underbrush. Some of them even crawled down the trunks of trees, their eyes appearing overhead like stars as they approached the pulsing light. Even the shadows that didn't host a pale, dead face had one or two pairs of eyes glittering off in the distance, watching from the dark. And once more, all of them were focused on the flashing stone, their expressions frozen as though hypnotized.

From out of the shadows marched Rochester Erickson, his ponytailed head held high and his cravat-ruffled chest puffed out. For a moment, he glared at Alec—and then his eyes landed on the bundle in Derek's arms.

"At last," he said, his voice filled with what Alec could swear was love. "The sleeper. We can begin."

20

SNUFFED OUT

Something about the tone of Rochester's voice shook Derek. Alec watched as the boy took a step backward and held Joan a little tighter. For his own part, the hunger in Erickson's eyes filled Alec with disgust now that he knew who and what the man really was.

"Samuel Gareen, I presume," Alec said.

A smile crept across Erickson's mouth, though he never looked away from Joan. "Samuel Gareen was the best man I ever knew," he said softly. "I'd like to think he's with us now, in spirit, to see this miracle performed."

"A miracle involving someone else's baby," said Alec, feeling anger redden his cheeks. "Those are always super legit. But I guess Ichthyon works in mysterious ways, huh?"

That one did it. Erickson turned and glared at him with those bright madman's eyes.

"And what do you know about the Master's wonders?" he said in a low rasp, his voice quivering in excitement. "What could a crawling, insignificant little *grub* like you know about the grandeur of a living god? A force so powerful that not even light could touch him, so that wherever he walked, darkness fell over the land and turned the people into his disciples. A god who promised to end all of humanity's woes and nearly did, were it not for the fearful men of his time!"

"Guess humanity's got no woes if everyone's dead," said Hannah.

Erickson chuckled. "A Maplethorpe to the end. Perhaps I will reward your bravery by letting you see the Master—or granting you a swift, painless death. Whichever you prefer."

"What?" asked Derek. He took another step back, but three scrabblers came crawling up behind him and snagged him in their long, wispy hands. He twisted and fought as best he could, but one of them yanked Joan from his grasp, while the others blasted him in thick gobs of gray slime from their backsides. Derek cried out, but the more he struggled, the more he gooped himself up in the stuff. Once he was thoroughly coated, the scrabblers went to work, spinning him between them and adding more slime as they went, until Derek was encased in a gray, sticky cocoon of sorts. The sight of them capturing him made Alec nauseous; he wondered if Checkmate would puke again.

"All that's left is the bezoar," said Erickson. He turned to Checkmate and held out a hand. "Give it here, my silent friend. No need for any violence."

Checkmate's beady, dark eyes narrowed. He held the stone away from Erickson and crouched as though ready to run or fight—and then the scrabblers were on him, wrapping their arms around his neck and legs. Checkmate thrashed as hard as he could, but there were just too many of them, and even as strong as he was, he couldn't break free of their grip.

"Don't touch it!" cried Erickson, panic making his voice crack. He darted forward and snatched the glowing stone out of Checkmate's hand. Then he turned and stared deep into it, the green glow rising and falling on his maniac grin. "Careful, my sweet pets. It is a powerful item. It would be your undoing if you were to touch it."

"Don't do this!" shouted Alec. "Please, Erickson—Gareen—whoever you are, all you're doing is killing innocent people!"

Erickson laughed, a sound as hollow to Alec as a stone rattling around in an empty can.

"All my life, small people have doubted me," he said. "They said I was *detached from reality*. But I have seen the world, child. I know its horrors. And unlike the lot of you, I have the power to end them." He turned to the scrabblers and swept an arm off into the forest, up the hill toward the Ridge. "Quickly, my children! To our sanctum! We've no time to lose!"

"No! Stop!" cried Alec, but already the scrabblers had thrown Checkmate to the ground and were scuttling off into darkness. Erickson held the stone high and marched off among them, the throbbing light growing dimmer with every step he took. At the end of the procession was Derek, carried away screaming by the scrabblers who had bound him in their slime—and then even he was gone, the crunching of footsteps and the flashing of the light growing smaller and fainter until it was entirely swallowed by the black.

Complete hopelessness crashed down on Alec, sending him to his knees. There they were, out in the woods, in the dark, with nothing to help them. It was like the blackout had overtaken his entire life, turned it into something vast and empty and hopeless.

They'd lost. They were doomed.

"Alec," sobbed Hannah off to his side, somewhere in the night. "Alec, we have to do something."

Alec swallowed over a dry mouth and said shakily, "There's nothing to do, Hannah. It's done."

"No!" she moaned. "No, Alec, he has my *sister*! We have to do *something*!"

All at once, the stress and effort of the past few days swept over him.

"There's nothing we *can do, Hannah*!" he shouted. "They have everything! Everything we did was for nothing! We *failed*! *Lost*! *We're DEAD!*" He shoved his hands to his face, clawed at his eyes, wrenched his hair, and screamed into the darkness. "I should've, I should've gotten on the ferry. I should've gone home, gone to live with my dad and stupid Suzanne. *He* wouldn't have ruined everything and failed everyone. *He* would've done something. *He* would've come up with a plan. He—he—"

"Your dad bailed, though, right?"

Alec froze, his anger vanishing in a flash of shock. The strange voice had come only a few feet away from him, deep and touched with an accent. He'd never heard it before—and yet somehow he recognized it immediately.

"That's the word around town, anyway," continued the voice. "That you guys moved to the island after he hit the road. That right?"

"Y-yeah," said Alec. He let out a long, tired breath and lowered his hands to his sides. "He . . . he moved in with his personal trainer. Suzanne."

"Right," said the voice. "So don't worry about him, because he bailed. Because he wanted to, or because he didn't feel like putting in the effort. But man, for the past few days? I've watched you and Hannah work your *butts off*, going the extra mile to try and figure out what the heck is happening around here. You're the hardest-working kids I've ever *seen*. So I get that you miss your pops—I'd miss him, too—but honestly? Seems like you're a lot tougher than him. And unless he can see in the dark, I'll take my chances with you guys over him any day. As long as y'all are on my team, we're not out of the game yet."

Alec swallowed, nodded, and climbed to his feet. "You're right. It's . . . it's going to be hard, but it's not over. There's gotta be something we can do." He wiped a tear from his face, reached out, and found Hannah's hand in the dark. "We're going to figure out a way to get your sister back. I promise."

Hannah sniffled and squeezed his hand. "Thank you, Alec," she said in a wet, cracking voice.

"What are friends for?" said Alec. He turned in the direction of the voice, and though he knew it was invisible in the dark, he smiled. "Thanks, Eli."

There was an awkward shuffling in front of him. "Checkmate will do," he mumbled.

21

REVELATION

This time, it was Hannah's nerdy science knowledge that paid off. As they were clawing around in the darkness, looking for broken sticks and ferns that would tell them where Erickson had stepped, she screamed, "It's furry here!" That's when Hannah revealed she'd been one of Founders' four Girl Scouts when she was seven—and that she'd found a patch of moss growing on the side of a tree.

"Moss only grows on the north side of trees,"

she explained. "When Erickson and the scrabblers left, they were heading northeast, toward the base of Hobble Ridge."

"We follow the moss, we get to them eventually," said Alec. "It's not the most foolproof plan, but it'll work for now."

"Well, it can't all be geology, can it?" said Hannah, and all three of them laughed in the dark. It felt good, Alec thought, to laugh in the face of all this disaster. Like a cup of hot cocoa, warming him from the inside.

They drifted from tree to tree, feeling for moss. All around them, the woods felt vast and strange; more than once, they heard the crunching footsteps of animals as they passed. They walked uphill, and the uneven ground and sudden rise of thick pine trees tripped all of them up once or twice. Eventually, they created a chain, with Hannah at the front feeling for moss, Alec in the middle holding her hand, and Checkmate bringing up the rear holding his. This way, they kept a straight path and held each other up when the footing became treacherous.

"Guys," said Checkmate after they'd walked for what felt like hours, but for all Alec knew had been a few minutes. "There, up ahead—I can just barely see it . . ."

Alec squinted—and realized Checkmate was right. The one upside of the complete depth of the blackout was that even the tiniest bit of light was visible, and a few hundred yards away, Alec could make out the outline of the trees through a soft, throbbing green glow.

The slope of the Ridge got steeper as they moved toward the light, forcing Alec to lean into the step and sending sweat down his back and arms. With every foot they hiked, the light grew a little brighter, drawing them in like moths to a porch lamp. Then, finally, they reached the tree line and burst out into a rocky clearing.

The light pulsed out of a cave mouth in front of them, and around it they could see the huge, looming shape of Hobble Ridge leaning over them. This close, Alec found the strange, swooping mountain even more intimidating than he had from afar; something about the way it disappeared and reappeared in the green glow was especially scary, as though the next time it was lit up, the Ridge might have somehow moved closer, preparing to crush him in the dark.

But it wasn't just the huge shape of the ridge. It was the cave itself, the way the stone seemed layered until it vanished into the ground. He'd seen a shape like this before—but not in his study of rocks.

"They're in there," said Hannah, sounding both determined and a little nauseous. "We've got to go into the cave."

"Last chance," mumbled Checkmate. "We could try 'n' go get help. Call the cops."

Alec exhaled long and slow. The idea sounded so tempting—go back to town, head home, hug his mom, call Officer Allander. Let someone else deal with it. In all honesty, he really did not want to go down in a glowing hole and fight giant crickets and the ghost of an old pioneer.

The choice, he knew, was up to him.

"Come on," said Alec.

The cave itself was a bottomless hole that went straight down, but a set of stairs had been carved into the stone edge, spiraling into the earth. The three of them began descending carefully, one shoulder against the wall at all times. The farther down they went, the brighter the light became, and the warmer the air. Soon, huge webby ropes of gray stuff—the slime, Alec thought, that the scrabblers gave off—stretched between the walls of the cave, forcing them to crouch under them or tiptoe over them. There was a noise, too, a deep humming that rose and fell with the pulsing light . . .

"Yo," said Checkmate, swatting Alec's arm with his big hand and pointing at the wall across from them. "Think that's our guy?"

Etched into the stone with deep, dark strokes was an illustration of a scene that made Alec's blood go frosty. Tiny stick-figure men held hands to form a circle, at the center of which was a huge black cloud, a smear of old paint or charcoal. Inside the giant smudge was the outline of a huge creature. Its body was hunched and hanging with what looked like hair, and it had a head somewhere between that of a whale and a crocodile. The beast had its huge, clawed fingers spread wide, and out from them erupted black veins of lightning that stretched across the stone.

At its center was a green ball . . . and a small wrapped bundle.

"That's him all right," said Hannah. "Come on, we need to hurry." They shuffled down the stairs even quicker, Alec doing his best not to look at the horrible, looming monster in the drawing.

Finally, the stairs reached the bottom, and a small passageway led to what sounded like their final destination. Hannah held a finger to her lips, and they tiptoed as silently as they could through the cave, crouching low so as not to be too visible in the pulsing green light. All the while, the humming grew louder, vibrating through the rock around them.

Hannah reached a point where the passageway opened up—and froze. She dropped down onto her stomach, motioning for the boys to do the same. Alec marine-crawled up to the edge with her, the rising and falling humming almost deafening at this point. Then he gazed out into the cave, and all noise seemed to fade out of the world, save the blood rushing in his ears.

The chamber was vast, the size of a church; their passageway let out some twelve feet above the floor. The walls were a webbed mass of gray mucus, and all along them crept scrabblers, bodies twitching and moving slowly while their pale, dead faces stayed completely focused on the scene taking place on the ground. One of them clung to the wall right below them, so close

Alec could see its hunched abdomen bobbing with the rhythm of the humming. They were the ones, Alec realized, who were causing the noise, their phlegmy voices joined in deep vibration that rose and fell with the glow of the stone. Among them, Alec spotted Derek glued to the wall with a mass of gray slime; some of the stuff had been slapped across his mouth, too, so that he could do nothing but watch the scene unfold.

In the center of the cave, Erickson stood before a stone altar that seemed carved out of the cave itself, or that had somehow been raised out of the stone floor. Baby Joan sat on the surface, still deep in her sleep with her tiny hands balled up beneath her chin; next to her lay a thick, old book, open and waiting.

You gotta give it to Joan, thought Alec. *She can sleep through anything.*

Erickson held the stone over his head, letting its light fill the chamber around him. And as it pulsed, something behind him glowed back.

A huge mass of flesh, about fifteen feet high, glimmered in the darkness behind Erickson. It was bulbous and slick, its surface lined with deep curlicues that spiraled in on themselves. Whenever the stone in

Erickson's hands pulsed with light, the massive pile of meat quivered, and bluish-green light seemed to flicker over the indented lines.

"What *is* that behind him?" asked Hannah. "It almost looks like . . ."

It hit Alec all at once—the fleshy mass, the strange brow of Hollow Ridge, the shape of Cathedral Rock. The cliffs, the gulch, all of it made sense. He remembered the island's outline in Robert Rector's journal, and he finally understood why the man had become so obsessed.

"It's brain matter," said Alec.

"*Brain* matter?" asked Hannah.

Alec nodded and admitted it both to himself and his friends.

"Founders Island isn't an island," he said. "It's a skull. Erickson's not trying to summon this monster from somewhere else—he's bringing the thing back from the dead. And we're inside of its head."

22

THE LAST NIGHT

"My children!" boomed Erickson, his voice echoing throughout the cave. "Our time is finally here! Freedom—from the daylit world, from the sins of humankind! Tonight, *Ichthyon will rise again*!"

The stone beneath Alec vibrated as the humming of the scrabblers rose in volume. He reached out and gripped Hannah to steady himself, only to find her shaking with fear.

"When he descended from the heavens, Ichthyon

brought with him an impenetrable cloud of glorious night," said Erickson. "All those who were touched by it became as you are now, servants in body and soul. But the shamans of that age could not accept the darkness and gathered together to destroy this beautiful annihilator before he could sweep the Earth clean of weak, pitiful human life. His death caused a mighty cataclysm, flinging relics far and wide. His skull became the land beneath us, while some portion of his mind reached the stars and orbited as a mighty comet bringing darkness and hope throughout our galaxy."

"Erickson's Comet," mumbled Hannah. "It's a piece of this thing's brain!"

"Between the cranium and the comet formed the sleeper," said Erickson. He lowered the rock to the altar and gently raised up Joan, who wriggled slightly in her sleep and yawned. If she woke up at all, they couldn't tell—the darkness of the cave was about as deep and impenetrable as that of the blackouts. "In her dreams, Ichthyon's halo of darkness spread out onto the world, and with it, my power—" Erickson seemed to pause, just for a moment, and then began anew. "*OUR* power has been restored! She is the gateway that will give us life again and will bring Ichthyon back into a world that so terribly needs him!

"The final piece has come to us," continued Erickson. "The bezoar, formed in the Master's belly, lost at his death. Before, it was broken in two, useless; now, made whole once again, its healing powers will bring Ichthyon back! By placing the sleeper and the bezoar together in our master's flesh, his body will be restored, and his spirit will be pulled through the gateway. Ichthyon has made me his herald, and now I will restore him to his former glory!"

"Some glory," whispered Checkmate, his brow furrowed in disgust. "These poor saps get turned into giant spricklets, while he gets to do all the yelling and preaching."

Alec nodded . . . and an idea popped into his mind, small and simple.

Then it grew, and grew. Like pieces of a puzzle, the facts he'd collected over the past few days connected and eventually formed a plan.

"We need to get the bezoar," he whispered.

"My *sister* is more important than a *rock*," hissed Hannah impatiently.

"If we get the bezoar, we get your sister," said Alec. "Trust me, I know what I'm talking about."

"Well then, lay it on us," said Hannah. "What do we have to do?"

"The first thing we need is a distraction." Alec considered the roles that all three of them would need to play for his idea to work . . . and his heart sank. He sighed. "Which I guess would be me."

"Are you sure?" said Hannah.

He nodded, absolutely hating what he was about to do. "Yeah, positive. Hannah, while everyone's distracted, sneak down there and grab Joan. Checkmate, when Erickson's off his guard, get that stone to me. Do whatever you have to. For now, just stay out of sight until the time is right."

"What're you gonna do?" Checkmate asked.

Alec looked down at the scrabbler clinging to the wall just below them and said, "This."

He pulled himself forward, slid out of the passageway's mouth on his belly, fell through the clammy cave air—

And landed on the creature's back.

Instantly, everything was chaos. The scrabbler

released a deafening howl and began bucking and thrashing beneath Alec, who clung to its abdomen like some sort of otherworldly rodeo rider. (It was warm, he noted with complete and utter revulsion; its shell was sticky and slick and *warm*.)

"Grab him!" shouted Erickson, and suddenly all of the scrabblers were rushing him at once, seizing him in their feathery claws and yanking him off their brother. Alec twisted and screamed and tried to fight off the desire to barf as some dozen giant bugs held him in their arms and dragged him up to the altar.

Erickson marched around the stone table to stand before him. His smug smile and purposeful stride told Alec that he thought he'd won. He held the bezoar up between them as though to taunt Alec with it.

"Young Master Zong," said Erickson.

"It's Xiang," said Alec, focusing on the smiling psycho before him and not the feeling of warm, feathery insect fingers on his face.

"It doesn't matter, really," said Erickson. "Soon, you will simply be one of the faithful, like my followers here. When Ichthyon's darkness spreads across the world, all will fall under his sway."

"Seems like a bad deal," said Alec. *Keep him talking*, he thought. *Give them all the time you can*. "But I guess that's the kind of stuff you learn when your dad raises you in a cult."

Erickson's smile slowly curdled into a grimace. "My father was a visionary," he said.

"Nah, he was—what'd people used to call you? *Detached from reality*," said Alec. "And it looks like he did a number on you. It's okay, Sammy—my dad sucks, too."

Erickson knelt slowly and stared unblinking into Alec's eyes. In his expression, Alec saw no emotion, not even rage—just cold, hard determination. It was more terrifying than any giant bug or ancient god he could imagine, and he wondered if this was it. If their journey was all over now.

"Before I feed this babe to the Master and usher in the new world," he said in a voice that shook ever so slightly, "I think I'll strangle you. And then I'll use this stone to bring you back to life so you can see your entire world fall into darkness."

Over Erickson's shoulder, Alec saw a shape crouch on the altar.

"That's one idea," he said. "But let me suggest something different. Checkmate?"

The sound of sneakers on stone rang through the air. Erickson's eyebrows went up, he spun, and—

CRUNCH! Checkmate leapt sideways and drop-kicked Erickson in the face. Erickson yelped and stumbled back, his arms wheeling.

Alec watched as the green stone flew out of his grip—and landed a few yards away, right in the middle of all the scrabblers.

"No!" shrieked Erickson, clutching his bleeding nose, but it was too late. The scrabblers went after the stone instantly, clicking and grunting with glee as they dog-piled onto it. Alec felt the dozens of hands release him as the creatures holding him went for the bezoar themselves

Over and over again, the same thing occurred— a scrabbler seized the rock, then screamed and fell to the floor, shaking violently. The pain their brothers and sisters went through didn't seem to bother the other scrabblers, who also picked up the stone, then dropped it and collapsed in a quivering heap. Soon, all the creatures lay spasming in the floor, until one by one they stopped moving, their spindly legs pointed at the ceiling.

A stench like rotten eggs filled the air, accompanied by a wet ripping noise.

The nearest scrabbler's body split down the middle in a gush of gray slime.

Out of it rose a woman. She was young, Alec saw, but had hard lines in her face that suggested a no-nonsense life. Her dress was plain and green, its hems bordered with faded lace, and her hair was an exploded mess, like she'd been shocked in a cartoon.

On her cheek, underneath her left eye, was a black tattoo of a key.

The woman held up her hands, looked at them with amazement, and whispered, "I'm me again."

"It's . . . it's really over." They turned to see another person rising from the carcass of a scrabbler, this one a bearded man in old sailor's clothes, his cheek also tattooed. One after another, each scrabbler's corpse cracked open and yielded up a human being. All of them were dressed in historic American garb. All of them marveled at their bodies, touched their faces as if to make sure they were real. All of them bore a key tattoo on their cheek.

As Checkmate helped Alec to his feet, the first woman to emerge looked at him, baffled—and then her eyes fell on Erickson, who was doing his best to crawl away from them.

"You!" she screamed, her face contorting in fury.

"Now, Sarah, try to remain calm," said Erickson, doing his best to summon his usual confidence—and failing.

The woman, Sarah, lunged forward with a shriek and seized Erickson by the collar of his coat, hauling him up to face her. He tried to wriggle free, but another one of the crew, a burly man with a long mustache and a coonskin cap, came up behind him and twisted his arm behind his back.

"How could you?" Sarah screamed, her face inches from Erickson's. "You promised us peace! Harmony! Utopia!"

"I made you something better than yourself, you miserable peasant," said Erickson, and Alec suddenly heard all lies and bravado leave the man's words, so that it was the oily voice of Samuel Gareen that spoke to her.

"You turned us into *monsters*!" she said. "You

tried to have us feed a sleeping babe to this unholy thing, and when we refused, you kept us prisoner in a living torture of eternal darkness! You told us your god would give us power, but the only one who was given any power was you!"

"The worthy shall always sit at the head of the flock," said Erickson, contempt dripping from his voice.

"Rochester, you are truly the worst man I've ever known." She shoved him away, and the burly man threw him to the ground. After a moment of staring at him in disdain, they turned to Alec and Checkmate.

"The babe," said Sarah. "The sleeping child. Is she safe?"

"She's okay!" All heads turned to Hannah, who held Joan safely to her chest to one side the altar. "Slept through the whole thing, if you can believe it."

Sarah nodded. "Then you must leave. Like it or not, the child and the beast are connected, and we know not how she will react to what we must now do."

"What are you going to do?" asked Alec.

His question was ignored. A girl, dark-haired and not much younger than them, came forward with the stone. She handed it to Checkmate and nodded sagely.

"Hide that somewhere safe," said Sarah. "Use it only when you must."

"You're not coming with us?" asked Hannah. "We—we could help you. You could live on the island, maybe even meet some of your descendants—"

"We cannot live outside of the darkness," said Sarah. "And that's as it should be. Our lives ended long ago. Tonight, we put a stop to this for good." She reached into the bust of her dress and pulled out a dagger, long and rusted. Then she turned to the room full of Founders Island's earliest settlers and called, "Friends! Take up your swords, your axes—whatever you bear! Tonight, *we slay the darkness once and for all*."

"What—no!" cried Erickson, his voice cracking in desperation. He reached pitifully for Sarah, but she kicked his hand away. Around them, the founders began drawing weapons—swords, knives, hatchets. One or two of them even broke off the stiffened legs of their old scrabbler bodies and brandished them like clubs. Then, with grim determination, they strode toward the pulsating mass of brain matter behind the altar.

"Who knew everyone was so heavily armed back then?" said Alec absentmindedly.

"We gotta go!" said Hannah, tugging at his arm. Alec snapped back into reality, and they began to head toward the mouth of their passageway . . . when Checkmate yelled for them to stop. He pointed to where Derek was slimed to the wall.

"I can't leave him!" said Checkmate, a look of sadness on his long face. "He messed up, but he's my friend."

Alec sighed, told himself he'd live to regret this—and then helped Checkmate pull Derek out of his gooey cocoon.

They managed to boost one another up to the passageway, handing Joan off as they went. While the other three ran down the tunnel, Alec looked back, taking in a last glimpse of the cave's unthinkable horrors. For a split second, he saw the first residents of Founders Island, hacking and stabbing at the mass of gelatinous monster brain as it quivered and gushed gray fluid—

"ALEC!" cried Hannah.

—and then he turned and ran.

Just as they reached the top of the stairs, a tremor moved through the ground beneath their feet. Out at the base of Hobble Ridge, they saw the woods illuminated—and not just by the light from the stone. Overhead, the comet was ablaze, flickering a nuclear green that bathed the entire island in strange light and long, grasping shadows.

"Look!" shouted Derek.

Hannah held Joan out at arm's length. The baby's eyes were wide open, flickering with green light that illuminated Hannah's expression of utter terror. Beneath their feet, the rumbling intensified.

Joan leaned back her head, opened her mouth, and released a deafening howl, like every scrabbler crying out at once. There was a crash and a gust of wind as the cave mouth they'd just left collapsed, huge stones pouring down and clogging the passageway. Overhead, the comet burned so bright that for a moment Alec thought he might be blinded.

Then, daylight.

Alec stepped back, blinking, and tried to figure out what had just happened.

The four of them stood in the shadow of Hobble

Ridge in broad afternoon light, each of their faces pale and frozen in shock. Around them settled a cloud of rock dust from the collapsing cave. Derek stared at baby Joan, so stunned he didn't seem to notice the huge clumps of gray slime hanging from his clothes.

Joan shifted in Hannah's arms. The little girl slowly opened her eyes, then smacked her lips and put her knuckle to her mouth.

"That . . . that means she's hungry," said Hannah with a little laugh of disbelief. "We should take her home and get her a bottle."

23

THE LIGHT OF DAY

"There. Do you hear it?"

Alec opened his eyes and watched Checkmate, wondering what he'd say. The huge boy's dark eyes popped open, but he just stared straight ahead, as though frozen.

"I think so?" he said softly.

"It's a heartbeat," said Hannah. "Almost like the universe's pulse." After a second, she added, "I think it could be cool behind a hip-hop track."

Checkmate's brow furrowed. "Oh."

"You can just say you don't hear it." Alec laughed. "I didn't hear it the first ten times." Hannah scrunched up her nose at him, and he held up his palm. "But—*but*—after a while, you start to notice it. It just takes time."

"Guess I gotta listen more," said Checkmate, his cheeks pinkening. He forced a little smile. "It's cool, though. Kinda like meditating. Thanks for showing me."

"No problem," said Alec, slapping the kid's huge, solid shoulder. There was no denying it—he liked Checkmate, liked the one-two of him being sturdy as a tree and shy as a dormouse. Ever since that night—or afternoon, during the blackout—in the cave, Eli Berger had become the third member of his and Hannah's crew, a looming pal whose warm heart came out more and more if you talked to him just right.

They sat a while longer, enjoying the sun and breeze. It was the first real summer day so far that year, and since the tourist season was starting late due to the blackouts—Mayor Friedmont had apparently proposed making this year's tourist campaign slogan A BRIGHT NEW FUTURE AHEAD! in order to combat rumors of the strange occurrences that had happened on Founders—they had the island to themselves for at least one more weekend.

Thinking about the mayor made Alec wonder how the town had done the mental acrobatics necessary to explain away the blackouts. The current line everyone was resting on was that the comet had somehow created a field of negative energy that blocked out the sun and caused an electromagnetic pulse that knocked out all the power. The green lights? Airborne algae. The weird howling? *Stellar winds*.

Alec had tried to explain to his mom and Mr. Jakka that there was absolutely no science to back any of that up—*stellar winds* was literally just a made-up phrase—but Mom was still mad that he'd bailed on the ferry without a word, and Mr. Jakka explained that comets were mysterious. It was Hannah who had finally told him to get over it. "You gotta remember how a small town works," she told him. "They need things to be normal. If you keep bugging them, they're going to worry that you'll bring back the blackouts."

It was the ignorant way to go—but, Alec thought as he breathed the salty air and savored the light on his face, he understood why the people of Founders Island wanted to forget. After the terror and emptiness of the blackouts, he'd started living like a lizard, spending all his time in the sun, absorbing daylight in huge quantities. Why ruin such a gorgeous day by dwelling on the darkness? Why think about the fact that they were sitting on a gum line, that Hobble Ridge was the bridge of an eye socket, that their whole lives were built on the skull of a monster, when you could just soak up some sun?

"Woof, it's later than I thought," said Hannah. "I gotta go home and get changed. We're still on for the movie, right?"

"Uh, yeah, of course," said Checkmate. As they climbed to their feet, he glanced at Alec. "Sure you don't want to come with? Day on the mainland's always fun."

"Nah, my mom's still upset with me," said Alec. "But I'll walk with you to Hannah's, if that's where you're heading."

Checkmate looked down at his feet. "Think Derek and I are getting a bite on the boardwalk first. He needs to get out of the house, away from his folks."

Alec sighed and shook his head. "You're a good dude for staying friends with the guy."

A hardness crossed Checkmate's face—not anger, but a kind of tough wisdom. Alec recognized it as the feeling behind the voice that had told him to soldier on when he was freaking out in the woods.

"Derek was the only kid brave enough to be my friend for the last four years," he said. "That's not something you forget."

Alec nodded. "Fair enough," he said, and slapped Checkmate five. "See you tomorrow. Enjoy the movie."

He and Hannah rode to the Honeycomb, where Big Gran sat on the front porch in a rocking chair, gently cradling Joan in her arms. She never looked up at them, but as Hannah and Alec climbed the stairs, a sour look crossed her face.

"Where you kids been?" she snapped. "Causing more trouble? Kidnapping babies and waving green lights around for the whole *dang* town to see?"

Hannah rolled her eyes. "Big Gran, don't be a hater," she said, and ran inside to change. Alec hung back and watched Baby Joan blow a spit bubble. From what they could tell, she'd come out of the experience totally unharmed—except for a small red blotch on her left cheek.

Alec peered closely at it. Did it look like a key?

"You leave this poor child alone," said Big Gran, glaring at him with her one milky eye. "Bad enough she has some curse on her. Now you gotta be treating her like a science experiment. It ain't right."

"Don't worry, I'm just glad she's okay," said Alec. "Besides, we don't have anything to worry about, Big Gran. The darkness is gone. We got rid of it."

Big Gran laughed once, hard—"*HANH!*"

"The darkness is still here, kid," she said. "We might not be able to see it most of the time, but it's always here, below the surface. This time around, it was this baby who opened it, but who knows what else could find it. That's what drove Bobby Rector out of his mind—knowing it was still here."

Alec felt the hair on his arms prickle. "You're saying it's a layer," he said, working the idea out in his head. "We're on the top . . . but the darkness is always underneath."

Big Gran nodded. "Well done. Makes sense, when you think about it. It hangs around him, like a cloud."

"Him?" asked Alec.

Big Gran squinted at him. "Well, it's *someone's* skull."

A breath hitched in Alec's lungs. He opened his numb lips to speak—

"All ready!" cried Hannah, leaping out of the door. The only thing more shocking to Alec than Big Gran's words was Hannah's outfit. She was rocking a sleeveless green T-shirt, an oversized orange zip-up hoodie, and cherry-red track pants, her look completed with high-top sneakers and too many bracelets. Her cheeks were smeared with glitter and her lip gloss shone like she'd put it on with a spoon.

"I think your outfit just burned a hole in my retinas," he said.

"This? This looks awesome," she said. "Act like a super-current mainland kid all you want, I know I look good."

"You look like a Spice Girl and a piece of sour candy had a baby," he said. "You look like Smartie Spice."

"Oh, shut up," she said, and then glanced at him from the corner of her eye. "The Spice Girls aren't still cool, right? That's not a thing I should know."

"Yeah, but in a retro nineties nostalgia way," he said, but he wasn't really paying attention. As they got on their bikes, all he could look back at was Big Gran's silent, dark expression. As they rode off, he glanced over his shoulder and saw her wiggling a long, bony finger in Joan's face, and the baby's chubby hands reaching up to grab it.

The path forked, and he waved Hannah goodbye as she veered toward the waterfront and he headed home. He could just see his house up ahead when his phone buzzed in his pocket. He pulled over to answer it.

"Hello?"

"Alec?"

"This is he," he said.

"Hey, kiddo."

Electricity shot through Alec. He stomped back on the brake, his bike skidding to an unbalanced stop.

"Hi," he said. "Hi, Dad."

"How are you?" his father asked, voice crackling due to the island's lousy reception.

"Oh . . . fine," said Alec. "Pretty much the same."

There was a pause, and then, "Well, listen, your mom has told me about some of the, uh . . . problems you've been having there of late. I was thinking maybe you should come back to the city. Stay with me for a while."

Alec blinked. He couldn't really comprehend the idea. "Stay with you. Back in San Francisco."

"Yeah," said Dad. "Back home. I know this has been tough for you, kiddo, but I never should've let your mom take you to some rainy little island. With everything happening, I wasn't thinking straight. I figure this way, you can go back to your old school, see your friends, and, you know . . . start life again."

The wind played with Alec's hair. He watched it move through the scraggly grass of Founders, over the hills, up by Marina Boulevard and off toward the northern edge of Hobble Ridge. He smelled the salt on the air, felt the sandy road crunch beneath his feet, watched a storm in the distance rolling gray and dramatic along the sea, just missing them.

"I'm good."

"Sorry?" asked Dad.

Alec frowned. Had he really just said that? His dad was giving him a chance to go back to everything he'd ever known—and, he thought, to move off what he now knew was the cursed skull of a dead demon.

This should've been a no-brainer . . . but in a way, it was. He'd answered without thinking, just feeling and knowing.

"Yeah, I want to stay here," he said, liking the way it sounded. "I have new friends here, and a new school, and I like it. It's nice out here. Maybe you can come out and visit Founders Island. I can show you around."

Dad sighed on the other end. "Alec, look, I'm sure you and your mom have had a real nice, uh, *adventure* out there. But come on, you've suffered enough. It's time to come home."

"I am home," he said. He heard Dad take a long, frustrated breath, and it stung. In the distance, Mom came out on their sagging front porch, spotted him, and waved. "I gotta go," he said, and then hung up and waved back before hopping on his bike.

His eyes snapped open.

No start, no sitting up with a sharp breath—just awake, for no reason.

It had been happening the last couple of days.

Alec rolled over and stared off into the blackness

of his room. The conversation with Dad ran through his head for the millionth time that night. He couldn't believe he'd blown off his father so quickly. For months, he'd wondered if he'd ever adjust to this weird community out in the middle of the ocean . . . and now, when the chance to go back to his old life had been floated in front of him, he'd brushed it away.

Part of it, he knew, was Hannah, and even Checkmate. He felt like he'd finally found his people, and even though they were unlike anyone he'd known back in the Bay, he finally felt like he belonged to something greater than himself. The out-of-touch headstrong lifer, the towering menace with a heart of gold . . . and the city kid with a secret love of rocks. It felt right, like he was completing a team.

But, he knew, it was also the adventure. Before he'd gone running around in the dark on Founders Island, he'd felt incomplete. There was always something he'd wanted—the newest phone, or the clothes that everyone was talking about. Now that he'd ridden a giant zombie bug inside the skull of a monster, all that stuff felt ridiculous. Now that he'd become a part of the legend behind Founders Island, he couldn't imagine leaving it. There was still so much to do, even if that just meant collecting rock samples and trying the boardwalk funnel cake everyone had told him about.

He yawned. It had to be late. He picked up his phone and pressed the home button.

Nothing. No light.

Alec's mouth went dry. The hairs on his arms stood at attention. Could it be? Were the blackouts already—

Wait a second, he thought. He reached around on the floor until he found his charger cable and plugged in the phone. An outline of his battery appeared, a red line at one end.

"Classic." Alec laughed to himself and put his phone back on the dresser. Then he rolled onto his side, closed his eyes, and finally let the darkness carry him away.

ACKNOWLEDGMENTS

It takes a creepy little cursed village to make a book like this happen, so here we go:

Massive gratitude to my editor, David Levithan, for bringing me on this project and for appreciating my pulpy weirdness. Thank you, sir.

My whole heart goes out to my wife, Azara, who listened to my hare-brained ideas about giant bugs and monster skulls. How she puts up with me, I'll never know. Thank you, my love.

Specials thanks to Arthur and Ivy, my niece and nephew, for teaching me about love, enthusiasm, patience, and raising a baby.

A bowed head for Captain Q, my grandfather, who taught me about the sea; and Kit Reed, my mentor, who taught me about the tide.

Finally, a tip of the fez to H. P. Lovecraft, without whose endless imagination and tragic prejudices this book would not have been half as interesting. Lovecraft was not a very open-minded guy, but his work is beautiful and weird, and reading it will better help you navigate the long darknesses of the world, if only by letting you know them a little better.

About the Author

Christopher Krovatin is an author and journalist whose YA and middle-grade novels include *Red Rover*, *Heavy Metal & You*, *Venomous*, *Frequency*, and the Gravediggers trilogy. His work at music outlets like *Kerrang!*, *Revolver*, and The Pit have resulted in wilder thoughts about Glenn Danzig than even he would care to admit.

Chris currently lives in New Jersey with his wife, Azara, and their son, Jacob. He would love to talk to you about Dracula.

Be afraid.
Be very, very afraid…